The Bear who Sailed the Ocean on an Iceberg

Emily Critchley

Published in the UK by Everything with Words Limited

Fifth Floor, 30–31 Furnival Street, London EC4A 1JQ

www.everythingwithwords.com

A CIP catalogue record for this book is available from the British Library.

ISBN: 978 1 911427 21 6

Printed and bound in Great Britain by

CPI Group (UK) Ltd, Croydon CRO 4YY

1

Patrick found the polar bear in the freezer on Sunday evening.

Tomorrow would be Patrick's first day back at school after the holidays and he had spent the afternoon helping his mum take down the Christmas decorations. Apparently, it was unlucky to have them up any longer.

She'd just asked him if he could take the heavy box of decorations and put them back in their place in the garage, in between the crate of old photography equipment, the bird-watching tent and camouflage netting belonging to Patrick's dad. Patrick had left the warmth of the kitchen, which still smelled of the spicy stew his mum had made for dinner, and let himself out of the back door. He'd run the few paces from the house to the garage. It was dark and cold out, and he only had his sweatshirt on.

He had struggled to open the back door to the garage one-handed. He could hardly see over the top of the box. The garage was freezing, as cold as outside. He'd fumbled for the dangling cord of the light switch, hoping he wouldn't touch a spider's web.

The large chest freezer they kept in the garage was open and inside was the polar bear. It must have squashed itself in there with some difficulty.

The door slammed shut behind Patrick and he dropped the box of Christmas decorations.

Patrick stared at the polar bear, unable to believe what he was seeing and, if he was being honest with himself, a little bit terrified.

He had never been this close to a polar bear before or, actually, this close to *any* bear before. He'd seen a brown bear once at Whipsnade Zoo but that bear had been quite far away, and behind thick glass. This bear was right in front of him. It had whitish fur, small ears, a large head and huge paws. Its nose was black and shiny. Patrick could only imagine how sharp the polar bear's teeth must be. He tried to think what he knew about polar bears. Weren't they carnivorous?

The polar bear opened its eyes.

Patrick looked at the polar bear and the polar bear looked at Patrick. The bear certainly didn't look much like a vegetarian. In fact, he looked hungry.

Exactly what a polar bear was doing in the freezer in the garage hadn't even occurred to Patrick. He was too busy shouting at himself in his head:

RUN!

Only he couldn't. His leg muscles felt tight and his arms were pressed into his sides. Something seemed to be gluing him to the spot. It was as if his feet had grown roots that were fixing him firmly to the ground, long tangled roots like the roots of the cress seeds he'd grown on cotton wool on the classroom windowsill in Year One.

The polar bear lifted one of his large front paws. 'Terribly sorry,' he said. 'I don't believe we've met.'

Patrick froze.

'A trifle stuffy in here,' the polar bear said, waving his paw in front of his face.

Patrick opened his mouth but no sound came out.

4

'I hope you don't mind,' the bear said, pointing to the floor. 'I helped myself to a few snacks.'

'S...s...snacks?' Patrick's voice sounded high-pitched and squeaky compared to the deep, booming voice belonging to the polar bear.

Patrick looked at the floor. He could see an empty packet of cod fillets and two empty boxes of chicken Kievs.

'They were a little crunchy, even for me,' the polar bear said. 'And I've known some cold fish in my time. Literally, I mean.'

Patrick nodded meekly.

'I was not referring,' the polar bear continued, 'to the common idiom meaning an unfeeling, hard-hearted individual, although I've known a few of those in my time too. The Atlantic walrus. Now, there's a cold fish. Shallow divers. Like to keep themselves to themselves. Paranoid too. Always think we're going to eat them, which I suppose we occasionally do.'

Patrick gulped. He wiped a shaky hand across his damp forehead. Here was a polar bear talking about eating walruses. Walruses were very large animals with big tusks. If the polar bear felt he could tackle a walrus for lunch, a twelve-year-old boy would surely not be much of a problem.

'The cat does seem to have got your tongue, rather, doesn't it?' the polar bear said. 'You do speak, don't you? Or do you just squeak? The Arctic tern. Now there's a squeaky bird. Always twittering on about this and that.'

Patrick made an attempt at clearing his throat. He didn't want the polar bear to mistake him for an Arctic tern. Did polar bears eat birds? Was there anything they *didn't* eat? This one seemed to like chicken Kievs.

'I'm sorry,' Patrick said, his voice coming

out clearer this time. 'I do speak. I guess I'm just not used to finding polar bears in the garage on a Sunday evening.'

'No one is much used to finding polar bears,' the polar bear said thoughtfully. 'We're an elusive lot. Except when we're hungry.' With that, the polar bear heaved himself out of the freezer and moved towards Patrick.

Patrick retreated in horror, flattening himself against the garage door. He felt something crunch under his trainer, probably a bauble. He shut his eyes, bracing himself for the white light and the cherubs with the tiny wings. He was about to become a polar bear's dinner.

Time seemed to slow down as Patrick waited for the end. He decided he'd had a short but fulfilling life. He'd seen England reach the final in the European Cup. He'd ridden the Vampire at Chessington World of Adventures and not been sick. He'd been runner up in the junior talent contest with his best friend Tommy Jenkins who had moved away in Year Six, even though their disappearing trick had gone wrong and the audience could see Tommy's toes sticking out from under the sheet they'd borrowed from Tommy's nan. Better than that, Patrick had won first prize in Year Four for the Peter Pan costume his mum had made for him on World Book Day. Luckily everyone had been too young to make fun of his green tights.

It hadn't been a bad sort of life.

As Patrick was thinking all this he realised he was still alive. Very slowly, he opened one eye.

The polar bear was standing in front of him, holding out a paw.

Patrick opened his other eye.

The polar bear didn't move, he simply held his paw out patiently.

He felt himself reaching for the polar bear's

paw. He wasn't able to shake it, exactly. He wouldn't have risked his fingers between the polar bear's claws. Still, it was a handshake of sorts. Patrick pressed his hand against the polar bear's large, padded paw and they moved their paws/hands in an up and down motion that resembled a handshake.

'It is customary,' the polar bear said, 'when making a preliminary introduction, accompanied by a handshake, that the two parties involved reveal their names.'

'Oh,' Patrick said. 'It's Patrick. Patrick Jolly.' The polar bear straightened himself. 'Wilbur Ambrose Cedric Barnaby Montague. The third,' he added. 'But most call me Monty.'

Patrick had never known anyone with three middle names. And he wouldn't have said the polar bear was a *Monty*. He looked like he should have a name that was more fierce, somehow, more suited to a polar bear. Maybe something like *Fang* or *Crusher*. Patrick supposed people didn't always suit their names. There had been a boy at his primary school who wore large square glasses and often had his jumper on inside out. His name was Bradley but Patrick had always seen him as a William. What sort of name would someone give to a non-threatening polar bear? He definitely didn't want to encourage the polar bear to be more fierce. He tried to think of something more cuddly, something a polar bear at a zoo might be called.

'What is it?' the polar bear asked.

'It's just, you don't really look like a Monty,' Patrick said, before he'd had time to think about it.

The polar bear frowned. 'Well, what would you have said then?'

'Snowy?' Patrick suggested.

'Snowy?' The polar bear raised an eyebrow. 'I can assure you I have never known a friend, relative or acquaintance called *Snowy*.'

'Sorry.'

The polar bear, or rather, *Monty,* sniffed loudly. 'Quite alright,' he said.

It was then Patrick remembered he was only supposed to be putting the Christmas decorations in the garage and that he had now probably been quite some time because of talking to a polar bear and all. He didn't want to worry his mum. She'd wonder what he'd been doing. The thought of telling his mum he'd found a polar bear in the garage was unthinkable. She had enough to worry about what with trying to feel better and Patrick's dad being away for work.

He supposed that when you found a polar bear in your garage, you should probably call someone. Tommy's mum had found a bat in their conservatory last summer. It had flown in through an open window. She'd called the twenty-four-hour bat hotline, only when she'd called, the line had been closed. The bat had stayed in the conservatory all night, hanging upside down on the curtain rail and pooing on the rug. It had eventually flown out sometime the next day. It was unlikely, he thought, that a hotline existed offering advice on what to do when you find a polar bear in your garage, twenty-four hours or not.

It was a good thing, Patrick thought, that his mum didn't come into the garage much. She said it was cold and full of spiders, which is why she'd asked him to put the Christmas decorations away in the first place.

'I was wondering,' Patrick said carefully, 'if you were planning to stay here tonight?'

'Oh, I should think so,' Monty said, loping casually back over to the freezer. 'In fact, I should think I shall stay for a while.'

'Oh,' Patrick said, his face falling. He wanted to make a suggestion as to where else Monty might go but, right at this moment,

he couldn't think of anywhere. It was getting late and he didn't think it was a good idea for a polar bear to be roaming the Hertfordshire suburbs after seven o'clock in the evening.

He had once heard about a lynx that had escaped from an animal park in Wales. The lynx, considered to be a threat to human life, had been shot. Patrick was pretty sure that if a large cat had been considered a threat to human life, a polar bear most definitely would be – whether he had a name or not.

Perhaps it would be best if he didn't call someone after all.

Another thought popped into his mind. He worried about his garage being so close to their next-door neighbour's house.

Most of the neighbours in Cherry Tree Close were very nice. Mr and Mrs Wilkinson and their three small children lived at number five. Mr and Mrs Abidi and their daughter Sanaya were at number eight.

Simon and Simon lived at number two with their dachshund, Rudolph. It was only Mr Crankly, Patrick's next-door neighbour, who was mean and grumpy. Patrick's mum said Mr Crankly had been in a war, only Patrick could never remember the name of the war. He thought it had something to do with forks.

He definitely didn't want Mr Crankly discovering there was a polar bear in the Jollys' garage planning to stay for a while. Mr Crankly would immediately alert the authorities. He'd know *exactly* who to call. He probably still had guns, or a bazooka, left over from the war.

'I was wondering,' said Monty, interrupting Patrick's thoughts. 'If you had any ideas about breakfast.'

'Breakfast?'

'You know,' Monty said, 'breakfast. The meal that breaks the fast. Most important of the day.'

Patrick realised that Monty was asking him what he should do for breakfast, as in what he should *eat*. He tried to think what a polar bear might like for breakfast. He was pretty sure it wouldn't be marmite on whole wheat toast which is what Patrick was planning to have tomorrow morning, or gluten-free muesli with goat's milk, which is what his mum would undoubtedly be having.

'I'm not sure there's much in for breakfast. But I can go to the Co-op after school tomorrow if you like? I might be able to get you some fish.'

Monty's eyes brightened. 'Fish. Yes, *fish*. Perfect. I should think I'll be able to hold on until supper time. Polar bears are quite used to fasting. Although I *am* known for being a little cranky at breakfast, not that I've ever perceived the trait to be a character deficit. "Only dull people are brilliant at breakfast," as Mr Wilde once said.'

'Mr Wilde? Was he an explorer?'

Monty chuckled. 'I shouldn't have thought so. "A place where birds fly around uncooked" was, I do believe, Mr Wilde's definition of nature.'

Patrick stared at Monty. Although he would never have expected to find a polar bear in the garage, especially not one who spoke, he *certainly* wouldn't have expected to find a polar bear who talked like Monty.

'Who exactly is this Mr Wilde then?'

'Why, Oscar, of course!'

Patrick must have looked blank because Monty stood up on his hind legs, which was pretty alarming, and proceeded to say, rather unnecessarily loudly, Patrick thought, 'Oscar Wilde! Poet. Playwright. Witty raconteur. Gentleman of the finest calibre. Most iconic and prominent figure in late Victorian society!'

'Sorry,' Patrick said. 'Never heard of him.'

16

Monty sighed and dropped back down onto four paws. 'Never mind. What I was saying is that I should be able to skip breakfast tomorrow if supper is to be provided.'

'Um, great,' Patrick said, thinking he might at least be able to sleep a little better knowing that Monty wasn't starving and could wait until Patrick got back from school. 'I'll see you tomorrow then.'

'Cheerio,' Monty said, waving a paw.

Patrick took several steps backwards, opened the garage door, and slipped outside. He shut the door firmly behind him then sprinted up the path to the kitchen.

2

The mud tasted of wet grass, old leaves, and rusty metal. He wasn't sure how he had ended up with mud inside his mouth but it must be there because he could taste it.

'Careful of that puddle there, Brolly. You might slip.'

Patrick lay on his stomach on the school playing field. He could hear the sound of Jake Sutherland's voice from somewhere above him, followed by the laughter of Luke Pierce and Caleb Nathan, two of the boys from his tutor group who hung around with Jake.

Patrick used to look forward to break and

lunch times, just like everyone else did. That was before starting secondary school last September, before Jake Sutherland started calling him Brolly.

'Have a good summer, Jolly Brolly?' Jake had asked meanly, causing the other boys to snigger and the girls to look away.

Jake would trip Patrick up in the corridors between lessons. He'd pushed Patrick against the lockers once at break time causing Patrick's shoulder to bruise. Jake also liked messing Patrick's hair up, dragging his grubby fingers through it. 'Just giving you a new look, Brolly,' he'd say.

Patrick's hair was thick and curly and it was hard to get it to stay flat, especially once Jake had messed it up. Patrick was small for his age and he supposed this made it easy for Jake to push him around.

Jake hadn't always been like this. At primary school Jake was just another boy who lived up the road. He liked football and athletics and danced with all the girls at the Year Six leavers' disco. Patrick had even been over to Jake's house once or twice because he had a big garden and two real football goals. That was ages ago though. Something had happened to Jake Sutherland over the summer holidays. He'd turned mean and his meanness seemed to be directed towards Patrick.

In Year Six, there had been lots of rumours about what secondary school would be like, rumours about the heads of Year Seven pupils being slammed into lockers or flushed down toilets by older boys. These rumours turned out *not* to be true. As far as Patrick could tell, the older boys weren't at all bothered about the younger ones. And why would they be? They had far more interesting things to think about, like their girlfriends or their important exams. The problem for

20

Patrick was the boys in his own year, in particular – Jake Sutherland.

Patrick opened his eyes and saw the red tag of Jake's new Kickers shoe next to his head. He closed his eyes. He had a horrible feeling Jake might stamp on him but when he opened his eyes again, the shoe was gone. Jake, Luke and Caleb were walking away.

Things would be different if Tommy were here and hadn't moved away to Bristol, to a school where they wore red blazers instead of blue.

His mum had been worried about Tommy moving. 'Have you made any new friends?' she'd asked him, that first week of school.

Patrick had shrugged. He didn't know how to tell his mum that best friends weren't replaceable like socks. You couldn't just go and buy a new pair if you lost one.

His mum had frowned. 'It's good to have a friend,' she'd said.

21

Patrick got up and wiped his trousers with the sleeve of his coat. It had rained heavily last night and the grass was wet. There was a large muddy stain on his right trouser leg meaning his school trousers would have to go in the wash tonight. *But I only did them yesterday,* he could imagine his mum saying. She still hadn't patched up his spare pair from where Jake had tripped him up in the playground last week. They'd torn at the knee where he now had a large scab. He'd told his mum he'd fallen over playing football.

There was no time to think about trousers now. The bell was ringing and Patrick had to get to class.

He went to his locker, grabbed his sketch book and pencil case, then made his way to the arts block.

Patrick liked art. He wasn't talented like Sammy Li who could draw manga so well

22

you'd think his drawings had come from the real comics. Patrick liked art because Mr Meer often let them work on whatever they liked, even though they were supposed to paint in silence. He would walk around the tables and advise them on how to make their work better, or else he would sit at the front of the classroom eating fruit from the fruit bowl that was supposed to be a prop for drawing. Patrick noticed Mr Meer often left orange peel or banana skins on his desk as if he were making some kind of modern art sculpture.

Today in art they were using charcoal. Patrick's class were allowed to take anything they wanted from the prop table to draw, or else they could borrow a book from the wooden bookcase, which contained Mr Meer's large and jumbled art book collection, and draw something from that.

When Patrick turned over a new page of

his sketch pad all he could think about was Monty. Had he really seen him? And not only seen him, but spoken to him? He hadn't had time to check the garage before school. His mum had already been in the kitchen when he'd come down for breakfast. She would have seen him slipping out the back door and asked what he was doing. He couldn't say that he was going to check and see if the polar bear was still in the freezer. His mum would probably take him to see Dr Benson, the family doctor, who had too much nose hair and who kept a creepy skeleton in his office. She would tell Dr Benson, in her worried voice, about Patrick's imaginary friends.

Patrick began to draw Monty exactly as he had first seen him: lying in the chest freezer with his paws sticking out. He drew Monty's shiny black nose and his furry feet. He added a few empty food packets to the garage floor

and a fish bone – just because he wanted to draw a fishbone.

'That's interesting, Patrick.' Mr Meer was looking over Patrick's shoulder.

'Thank you, sir,' he mumbled.

'Is it some kind of bear? And what's that box?'

'It's a polar bear, sir. In a freezer.'

Patrick could hear sniggers coming from the table behind where Jake, Luke and Caleb sat.

'Brolly's drawing a zoo.'

Mr Meer appeared not to have heard Jake's comment. 'It's very – abstract, Patrick,' he said, before moving on to Rebecca Hay who was drawing a vase and an old wine bottle.

Sammy Li looked across the table at Patrick's sketch pad. 'A polar bear in a freezer, that's cool. Ha, ha. *Literally*.'

'Thanks.' Patrick began shading in Monty's fur.

A compliment from Sammy Li was a bit of a result, someone who was actually good at art and took it seriously, unlike Jake and Caleb who were flicking bits of charcoal at each other when Mr Meer wasn't looking.

Patrick liked Sammy Li. Sammy had started school just a few weeks before the end of last term. He'd recently moved to the area. Patrick sometimes saw him cycling past the shops in the mornings. Patrick was also close enough to walk or cycle to school, as was Jake who lived with his parents and his older sister, Lily. Jake, unfortunately, lived just one street away from Patrick on Windmill Road.

Sammy Li was Chinese. He'd not only lived in China, but in America too. Patrick knew this because he'd heard the others ask Sammy about his accent which was kind of Chinese, American and British, all at the same time. Sammy liked to wear brightly coloured socks. He was kind of cool.

'How's that zoo coming along, Brolly?' Jake called out. 'Drawn any monkeys yet?'

Caleb snorted with laughter then began making monkey noises.

Mr Meer frowned at Jake's table. 'Settle down boys. Or I'll have to separate you.'

Patrick looked at the clock. The day seemed to be going on forever. He wanted to get home. He wasn't sure what would be worse, if Monty was still there, or if he wasn't. If he was there, well, that would involve a whole set of problems. If he wasn't, then maybe Patrick should take *himself* up to see Dr Benson.

3

Patrick stood in line at the checkout queue in the Co-op, holding his basket of fish. He had two packets of smoked mackerel and ten tins of sardines. He thought it best he didn't go into the garage without bringing Monty food. He had, after all, promised Monty he would get him some fish and he didn't want to break a promise he'd made to a large, hungry, walrus-eating polar bear.

He hadn't realised how expensive fish was. At first, he'd picked up three packets of salmon fillets but he'd put them back after

realising that they cost two weeks' worth of pocket money. Monty would have to make do with the mackerel and tinned sardines.

He heard laughter from the other side of the shop and realised Jake, Caleb and Luke had just entered. There was a sign on the front door stating that school children were only allowed in one at a time. Clearly Jake, Caleb and Luke thought these rules didn't apply to them.

The woman in front of Patrick appeared to be buying the whole shop. He watched as she stuffed frozen pizzas, bottles of bleach and packets of loo roll into her large reusable carrier bags.

He turned around and saw Jake, Luke and Caleb sloping into the Pic n' Mix aisle. They were filling a bag with sweets. He watched Caleb put a jelly snake straight into his mouth which made the others laugh.

Patrick realised he was breathing quickly. His mouth felt dry.

'Can I take those for you?'

The woman behind the checkout was pointing at Patrick's fish as the lady with all the bags shuffled towards the doors.

'Yes. Thanks.' The fish tins tumbled out of his hands and onto the conveyor belt.

'Fish for tea?' the woman asked, smiling at him.

'Um. Yeah.' Patrick coughed, clearing his throat.

'Good for the brain, fish,' the woman said, inspecting the packet of smoked mackerel. 'Did you know St John's Wood is the only Tube line that doesn't contain any letters from the word mackerel? I saw that on a quiz show once. It stuck with me.'

Patrick nodded politely. He wondered if she could possibly scan any more slowly. He didn't want to be talking about quiz shows

and Tube lines, he just wanted to get out before Jake saw him.

It was too late. Patrick glanced towards the Pic n' Mix aisle. Jake was nudging Luke with his elbow and pointing straight at Patrick. Jake moved towards Patrick whilst Luke and Caleb followed. They approached him the way lions might circle a quivering antelope. Although, wait, that analogy made *him* the quivering antelope.

'Look, there's Brolly! Got anything we can share, Brolly?'

'Need a bag, love?' the woman behind the checkout was saying.

'No, thanks.' Patrick shoved the fish into his rucksack but it was too late, Jake had seen what he was buying.

'What's with all the fish, Brolly?'

Jake was standing so close to him he could smell Jake's Lynx deodorant.

Patrick had always been terrible at lying

but even he knew he couldn't tell Jake he was buying fish for the polar bear he'd found in his garage last night.

'They're for my mum,' he muttered. He tried to concentrate on giving the checkout woman his four pounds and twenty pence. He would *not* be the quivering antelope.

'Aw. He's doing the shoppy woppy's for mumsey wumsey.'

Ignoring Jake, Patrick zipped up his rucksack and quickly exited through the Co-op's sliding doors.

'Hey, Brolly, enjoy your fishy wishys!' Jake's voice followed Patrick out of the shop.

'You forgot your receipt, love,' the checkout woman called after him.

'I'll give it to him,' he heard Jake say.

Patrick walked quickly along the road without looking back. His hands were sweaty and there was an empty feeling in the pit of his stomach. He didn't want Jake to catch up

with him. He didn't care about the receipt. He was almost running now.

'Oi, Brolly. Come back here. We only want to give you your receipt,' Luke said.

Jake laughed. 'Yeah slow down, Brolly!'

Patrick ran along the road, past the hairdressers and the fish and chip shop. He could hear Jake, Luke and Caleb running after him. He heard a scuffle.

'Watch where you're going, you clumsy oaf!'

Patrick turned and saw that Jake had bumped straight into Mr Crankly who had stepped out of the post office. Mr Crankly's bushy white eyebrows were knitted together and he was glaring at Jake.

'Pick that up!' Mr Crankly pointed at the receipt Jake had dropped.

'It isn't even mine,' Jake mumbled.

Mr Crankly folded his arms across his chest. 'I said pick it up! I didn't fight for this country so scallywags like you could come along and turn my neighbourhood into a pigsty. I bet it was you who put that crisp packet in my rose bushes last week!'

Patrick watched as Jake bent down to pick the receipt up. He didn't wait to see anymore. He was glad it was Jake, not him, who had bumped into mean Mr Crankly, and that Jake wouldn't be able to catch up with him now. He hurried off, around the corner, towards Cherry Tree Close and the relative safety of a hungry polar bear.

Patrick felt tired. School was tiring because he was always on edge, always wondering if Jake would be waiting for him around the next corner. He knew that things shouldn't be like this for him at school, yet he didn't know how to make Jake leave him alone. He thought he should probably tell someone Jake was picking on him but he worried it would

34

only make things worse. He could imagine Jake waiting for him after school, sneering at him, calling him a squealer or a snitch. Patrick wanted to tell his mum, but then she would only worry and he didn't want her to worry. Not now.

If this had happened last year, before *It* happened, he would have told her. Patrick's mum would have figured out a way to make everything okay again because that's what she always did, like when he was eight and he went away to Scout camp and worried he wouldn't be able to sleep, and his mum told him it was okay to hide his stuffed rabbit, Mr Nutkins, inside his sleeping bag. Or when he was nine and had forgotten to do that school project. His mum stayed up late making a Saxon helmet and shield out of cereal boxes and tin foil. But Patrick wasn't a little kid anymore. He couldn't ask his mum for help with Jake Sutherland. Besides, he was supposed to be looking after his mum, not the other way round.

When Patrick reached his house, he opened the front door and called out, as cheerfully as he could, 'Hi Mum, I'm back.'

'Hi, Patrick,' came his mum's mumbled reply from the living room. Patrick's heart sank. She didn't sound good today.

He kicked his shoes off and hung his coat on the peg rail. He looked for signs his mum had left the house. If she'd been for a walk along the canal her wellies might be muddy. They weren't. Her coat was hanging neatly on the peg rail, just where it had been when he'd left for school that morning. At least his mum was in the living room and not the bedroom. That was something.

Patrick's mum had been off work for quite a while now. Everyone said the only thing that would make Patrick's mum better was time. He heard it from everyone, from his dad,

from his nan, from his Aunt Pru in Dorset. *Time is the greatest healer. Give her a little time. Things will get better, in time.*

No one had told Patrick exactly how much time would be needed. At first he thought they were talking about weeks. Then he realised they meant months. Now he was terrified they were actually talking about years. Patrick had been wanting to bring the subject up again with his dad but he hadn't wanted to say the wrong thing, and now his dad had gone away for work and talking about it on online would be even harder than talking about it in real life.

A few months ago, Patrick had been going to have a sister, only she had come too early and had died just a few hours after she'd been born. Her lungs hadn't finished growing. They didn't have the special coating they needed and she couldn't breathe properly which meant she'd had to be given extra oxygen. She'd had something that began with a B. Patrick had trouble pronouncing it. It sounded a bit like a type of dinosaur and it had a dys–plas–see–ah bit at the end.

If he was being perfectly honest with himself, when his mum and dad had first told him he was going to have a brother or sister, he hadn't been at all sure he wanted one. It had always been the three of them. People said silly things about only children, that they didn't know how to share, or that their parents spoiled them. Patrick knew his mum and dad thought this was all rubbish, and he did too.

Tommy had a younger brother, Freddie, and Tommy was always coming into school with bruises on his shins from where Freddie had kicked him under the table at dinner. Tommy couldn't kick Freddie back as, being the eldest, Tommy would be the one who got into trouble. Being kicked on the shins under

the table at dinner didn't sound like much fun. Besides, Patrick's dad had always said having one child was better for the planet, along with remembering to do the recycling and drinking from reusable water bottles.

Then his mum had told him he would be getting a sister. At least, Patrick had thought, a brother could have helped him with his Lego Technics or played in goal in the garden, but a sister? What would he do with a sister?

'She'll still be able to do all those things,' his mum had said. 'Who knows, she might be better in goal than you are.'

Patrick didn't mind too much about this as his position was centre midfield. But then she had died and so now nobody would ever get a chance to find out. His mum and dad had been so sad it was as if they'd forgotten they still had him. His dad seemed to be getting better but his mum seemed to be getting sadder. She'd not gone back to work and she rarely left the house. For a while, she'd stayed in her pyjamas all day. Last weekend Patrick's dad had gone away for work so his mum now had to do more things, like cooking and washing and shopping. Patrick hoped this would remind her she still had him, that he still existed. He was sure his mum only got up and dressed and did all these things for his sake. Although it was nice that she did, Patrick wished she would get up and dressed for her own sake, not just for his.

Patrick took his rucksack into the kitchen. He'd go and sit with his mum in a minute. Right now he had a polar bear to feed.

4

Patrick opened the garage door slowly and peeped round. Monty was on top of the freezer, sleeping. Patrick hoped that he could leave the fish as a sort of offering then run away. He winced as he undid the zip on his rucksack as quietly as he could, then slowly slid the fish from his bag.

Monty opened an eye. 'Ah,' he said. 'Snackeroonies. Excellent.'

Patrick sighed then moved carefully towards Monty. He began handing some of the fish over like he was delivering stolen goods. He watched as Monty used one of his claws to pierce the plastic packaging. The smoked mackerel fillets disappeared into Monty's mouth very quickly.

'Hm. Interesting flavour.'

'They're smoked.' Patrick said. 'They're supposed to have been held over fire or something although Mum reckons they cheat and just add E numbers to give it a flavouring.'

'How strange. Perfectly delicious though.' Monty licked his lips and started on a sardine tin, hooking a claw through the ring and pulling back the lid. He pushed his tongue into the tin and swept out the entire contents in one lick. Patrick's mum was always telling Patrick to slow down when he ate and Patrick almost said this to Monty, but he stopped himself just in time.

He did think, though, that whilst Monty seemed happy and had a relatively full stomach, it might be a good time to ask him a few things.

'I was wondering,' Patrick asked, 'how you got here?'

Monty swallowed. 'I swam, of course.'

This was not the answer Patrick had been expecting, although he wasn't actually sure what he had been expecting. 'That must have been tiring.'

'Oh, it wasn't too arduous,' Monty said, licking a piece of sardine from his left incisor. 'Once I got out of the river and up the waterways, it was fairly quiet. I think I may have frightened the locals though.'

'What do you mean?' Patrick asked, alarmed. He dropped the last of the sardine tins he was handing over.

Monty chuckled to himself. 'They didn't half get themselves in a tizz. Flapping and quacking. I tried to initiate conversation but they weren't having any of it, although I suppose my duck is a little rusty.'

Ducks.

Patrick let out a deep sigh of relief as he reached to retrieve the dropped tin. 'You mean the ducks were the only ones who saw you?' he confirmed.

'Yes. I'm afraid to say I may have startled the resident waterfowl.'

'I bet. Do you mean you swam here up the canal?' He passed Monty the dented tin and watched as Monty hooked a claw into the ring-pull and peeled back the lid.

'Very useful. Canals. The modern canal system is a product of the Industrial Revolution, of course. Superseded by the railway. I didn't swim all the way,' Monty said, 'from Greenland. The waterways were only the final furlong, you see.'

'I see,' Patrick said, not really seeing. 'Then how…'

'Well…' Monty sniffed. 'I am partial to a little doze now and then. Being rather mature in polar bear years.'

Patrick nodded.

'So, I settled down as usual on the icecap for my afternoon snooze. I was having a lovely little dream about a rather tasty seal but, when I woke, the piece of ice I'd been sleeping on had broken clean away. I had no idea where I was. It was terribly inconvenient. I was floating on a small raft of ice. Well, I boldly captained my icy craft for a number of hours but we drifted into warmer waters where my little boat began to melt. I was eventually left with only a tiny piece supporting my behind until, eventually, I plopped into the sea in a most undignified manner. I was forced to swim for a considerable amount of time, meeting only a common harbour porpoise who confirmed my geographical coordinates as the North Sea. By a stroke of luck, I came across a large ship. I hauled myself up on board, using a bit of rope someone had left carelessly dangling. I was quite fatigued by then so I settled down behind some crates for forty winks and woke up in the metropolis itself.'

'The metropolis?' Patrick asked.

Monty waved a paw in the air. 'London,' he said. 'You know, fish and chips. Cups of tea. Pigeons. The Queen.'

'Yes, of course I know London,' Patrick huffed.

Monty squeezed his large frame back into the chest freezer and settled himself down.

'Well, I think I'll just get a little shut-eye. Thank you for the snacks. That should keep me going until tomorrow.'

'You're welcome,' Patrick said, backing out of the garage. Clearly this meant he was going to have to come up with more fish for Monty tomorrow. He thought about explaining to Monty that it might be difficult to get him food as he had spent most of his pocket money. Not only that, but Monty didn't seem to have any idea how much danger he was in being so close to so many humans who, the minute they saw him, would perceive him to be a threat to their lives. Did he realise he couldn't stay here for long? That he shouldn't be here at all? Did he know where he was going to go from here or how he was going to get home? It was too late to ask. Monty was already snoring.

5

The following morning, after making breakfast for his mum and taking it upstairs for her, Patrick left for school. He crept around the side of the house to the garage and peeped through the keyhole. He could see Monty asleep in the freezer. It was probably best not to wake him.

When he reached the bottom of the drive, Patrick noticed Mr Crankly was in his front garden in his dressing gown and slippers. He was staring at his lawn and frowning.

Mr Crankly was retired, and lived alone.

He hadn't always lived alone. There had once, a long time ago, been a Mrs Crankly.

Mr Crankly wore a large white moustache and all his hair was on the sides of his head instead of on top. He'd lived next door for as long as Patrick could remember. He drove a dark blue Mondeo and he never put any lights up at Christmas. Even Mrs Furrows, who was eighty-two and who had the bungalow on the corner with the gnome-filled front garden, put an additional gnome dressed as Father Christmas on her step each year.

Mr Crankly's front garden was the neatest in Cherry Tree Close, possibly in the world. He had a small square of very green, immaculately mowed grass, a white fence, and a low privet hedge that separated his garden from the pavement. Patrick's dad liked to joke that Mr Crankly measured each blade of grass with a ruler to make sure they were all the same height.

To the left of Mr Crankly's lawn were his prized rose bushes. There were no roses now, of course, it was too cold, but in the summer Mr Crankly would be out the front with his pruning sheers and clippers, and a little spray bottle of water, trimming and spritzing his flowers.

Mrs Wilkinson from number five called Mr Crankly "The Rose Whisperer". *I don't know how he gets them like that,* she'd say.

Most of the neighbours in Cherry Tree Close would smile when they saw you, or wave hello. Not Mr Crankly. He only scowled or muttered grumpily under his breath. Once, when Patrick was small, he had been riding up and down the road on his new bike. Mr Crankly had come out and shouted at Patrick calling him Pipsqueak, saying that he was being too loud when his poorly wife was trying to sleep, and that his bike was making cracks in the pavement.

'That's rubbish,' Patrick's mum had said when he'd told her. 'Those cracks have been there since before you were born. Bikes can't crack pavements. But perhaps you'd better come inside if Mrs Crankly is sleeping.'

Patrick remembered how, last summer, someone on Cherry Tree Close had called the police, complaining of loud and raucous behaviour coming from the Wilkinsons' house. Apparently a party had gotten out of control.

'But it's three in the afternoon!' Mrs Wilkinson had said when the police arrived. 'Amelia is only four years old!'

Still the bouncy castle had had to be deflated and the birthday candles responsibly extinguished.

Patrick had always suspected it was Mr Crankly who called the police.

He had once seen Mr Crankly throw a boot at Tinkerbell, the Wilkinsons' cat, after she'd foolishly strayed onto his lawn. Tinkerbell was very white and fluffy and had one of those faces that made her look like she was always grumpy, although that day she'd had reason to be.

Last year, Patrick had caught a glimpse of the inside of Mr Crankly's house. His mum had signed for a package and had asked Patrick to drop it round. He hadn't wanted to go but his mum had insisted. He'd rung the doorbell which had played a buzzy, out of tune version of God Save The Queen.

Mr Crankly had opened the door and given Patrick a cold, hard stare. Patrick had caught a glimpse of the living room behind Mr Crankly. It had been very tidy. He had stripy wallpaper and a small, very old, TV.

Mr Crankly had snatched the package from Patrick, muttered something that *might* have been a thank you, and slammed the door.

52

Once, Patrick had accidentally kicked his football into Mr Crankly's back garden. He'd seen it disappear over the wall from the force of his rather superb kick.

Mr Crankly's back garden was just as tidy as the front: a neatly trimmed green lawn, small round bushes, a greenhouse full of tomatoes, lots of flowers, and a pond full of koi carp with a water feature and a statue of a boy weeing into the water. Patrick thought the statue was funny but his dad said it was a famous Belgian landmark.

Patrick had been too scared to go and ask Mr Crankly for his ball back. The next day he had found his ball pierced on one of the iron spikes on top of the garden wall. He'd fetched the ladder, climbed up, and retrieved it. He'd tried to patch the ball up with his puncture repair kit but it was ruined.

'Maybe it landed there?' his mum had suggested.

Patrick knew his ball hadn't landed on a spike. Mr Crankly had put it there after he'd found the ball in his garden. It was a warning, like the severed heads on spikes that used to be displayed on London Bridge as a warning to anyone else thinking of betraying the king. Patrick had learned about them on a school trip last year.

Now, as he was leaving for school, Mr Crankly was outside in his slippers standing on his path looking at something on his front lawn. He bent down to inspect whatever he was looking at from a closer angle.

Patrick could see that Mr Crankly was holding a ruler, one of those old-fashioned wooden ones. Maybe Patrick's dad had been right. Perhaps Mr Crankly really *did* measure his blades of grass!

As he got closer, Patrick could see that Mr Crankly wasn't measuring blades of grass at all. He was measuring a very large paw print

that had flattened a patch of his perfectly mowed lawn. The paw print was about the size of a polar bear's.

Mr Crankly looked up and scowled as Patrick passed.

'This one of your pranks, young man?' He stood up and waggled the wooden ruler at Patrick, the tops of his ears turning red.

'No,' Patrick said. 'I…I don't know anything about it.'

Mr Crankly scowled again.

Patrick wasn't going to hang around for a response. He turned and walked, almost ran, in fact, to the end of Cherry Tree Close. There was no predicting what a crazy old man with a wooden ruler   might do, especially when his lawn had been trampled by a polar bear.

6

As he walked to school, Patrick felt guilty about leaving Monty. But what could he do? He couldn't stay off school. His mum would know immediately that he was faking a cold. She was one of those mums who could always see through things like that. At least Monty seemed to spend a lot of time asleep. Hopefully he'd sleep in the garage all day until Patrick got home and could figure out what to do.

Later, in registration, whilst the others at his table were discussing who might win the

FA Cup Final this year, Patrick decided to make a list of all of his problems.

His mum used to make a lot of lists. She made lists for everything: shopping lists, meal lists, holiday lists, work lists, household chores lists. She said having things out of her head and down on paper made her feel less anxious and helped to organise her brain.

Patrick's list looked like this.

Patrick Jolly's problems:

1. Mum still sad.
2. Jake Sutherland
3. Monty
4. Mr Crankly discovering Monty
5. *Anyone* discovering Monty
6. Feeding Monty
7. Dad away (unable to help)
8. Need to get some more Odour Eaters for P.E. trainers

The bell rang and Patrick had to get to Geography. He tucked his list inside his homework diary and left the classroom with everyone else.

Mr Eddy wore colourful cord trousers and sweatshirts with the names of universities on them. Patrick didn't mind Mr Eddy, or Geography, even though they had to sit boy, girl, boy, girl. He sat next to Sara Hassan who was mostly quiet and did her work unless you got her on to the subject of German Shepherds. She had two; Mina and Tilly, and her aunt bred them. There wasn't much about German Shepherds Sara didn't know. They were apparently first used to aid the blind before Labradors took over.

Patrick sat near to the window. Outside, it was raining; one of those heavy, fat drop kinds of rain that always seems to come from nowhere. A group of Year Eights lined up outside the sports hall for P.E. were getting

soaked as Mr Larson, the P.E. teacher, shouted at them from beneath his large golf umbrella.

Mr Eddy was talking about climate change. He was explaining that because humans had burned so much coal and oil (Patrick already knew these were called fossil fuels) and cut down so many trees, gases were being trapped in the earth's atmosphere causing the planet to be warmer. He showed them photographs of the melting ice caps. Patrick thought of Monty.

'What's wrong with it getting warmer, sir?' Luke asked from the back row. 'I like the beach. My legs look good in shorts.'

Jake and Caleb laughed. No one else did.

Mr Eddy smiled. 'Warm weather doesn't just mean more trips to the beach, I'm afraid. It could mean forest fires, hurricanes, floods, a lack of food. And, anyway, there may not be so many beaches for you to go to.' He tapped the large map of the world on the classroom wall with his board pen. 'Shanghai in China, Osaka in Japan, Rio de Janeiro in Brazil, Miami in America, could all be underwater one day.'

Patrick knew about this already as his dad was often taking about climate change, along with them being in the middle of *The Sixth Mass Extinction*.

Apparently, according to Patrick's dad, there have been five other mass extinctions in the history of the planet due to ice ages or volcanoes. The last one was caused by a huge space rock that smashed into the Gulf of Mexico sixty-five million years ago killing off all the dinosaurs and a whole bunch of other animals, insects and weird fishy creatures along with them.

The Sixth Mass Extinction, the one they were supposedly living through now, hadn't been caused by any of those things, it had been caused by global warming which

kind of sucked really, if you thought about it.

Monty was already endangered enough. Patrick had to figure out a way of keeping him safe whilst he figured out how to get him home. Knowing Monty was in his garage was causing him to feel more and more worried. He was finding it hard to concentrate on anything else. What if Monty escaped and hurt someone? It would be all his fault. He knew Monty was there, in *his* garage, and yet he hadn't told anyone. Also, what if someone hurt Monty? That would be his fault too. He didn't know which would be worse.

He sighed and opened his exercise book. He was supposed to be copying something from the board. Sara was way ahead of him, scribbling furiously with her fluffy pink pen. He looked out of the window, at the wet playing field and the road behind which eventually led home to Cherry Tree Close and, now, to Monty.

His mum sometimes said he looked like he had the weight of the world on his shoulders. He could imagine her saying it now if she saw him. Luckily, she couldn't. And, anyway, she had her own problems. He certainly wasn't going to give her any more.

7

Second lesson was Maths with Mr Carson. In Maths, Patrick sat next to Sammy Li. They often sat next to each other, or on the same table, as their surnames were close together in the alphabet. There were no K's in Patrick's tutor group.

Mr Carson was in a bad mood. He complained that they had entered the classroom too noisily and made them all go outside and line up again. Patrick felt something swipe the back of his head.

'Ouch.' He touched his head and turned around. Jake was grinning at him.

'Just getting rid of that bit of dandruff, Brolly,' Jake hissed in a low whisper.

Patrick was about to say something but then Mr Carson was there.

'Patrick Jolly, you're facing the wrong way. And there's no need to hold onto your head. It won't fall off.'

'Sorry, sir,' Patrick mumbled. He could feel his face turning red.

Once they had all filed back into the room and sat down, Sammy whispered to Patrick, 'Jake's such a wombat.'

'Yeah,' Patrick said, opening his pencil case.

Jake was sitting next to Caleb at the back by the radiator. He somehow always managed to get a good seat.

'Hey,' Sammy said. 'What would you rather have, toes for fingers, or fingers for toes?'

Patrick frowned, thinking. 'I guess fingers for toes because then I could pick things up without having to bend down.'

64

Sammy was about to reply but Mr Carson scowled in their direction then tapped the instructions on the whiteboard with his pen and ordered the class to begin.

Patrick started working on the sums on the board. There was no use worrying about Monty right now. He'd just have to wait until he got home and hope that Cherry Tree Close hadn't been cordoned off with cones and police tape, and that if it had he wouldn't be held responsible.

The sums were the ones you needed to do with a calculator. After a few minutes he noticed Sammy was flicking his pen against his forehead and frowning.

'What's the matter?' Patrick whispered.

'I've forgotten my calculator.'

He knew what Sammy was thinking. Mr Carson hated people not having the right things in their pencil cases. He was known to give detention for it. Aaron Burns had forgotten a ruler, a compass *and* a pen a few weeks ago and Mr Carson had shouted at him and called him a name beginning with *I* that Patrick couldn't remember. It had sounded like *iguana mouth* but maybe a bit longer. He didn't think it actually was iguana because that was a type of lizard, although, thinking about it now, Aaron Burns *did* look a *bit* like a lizard. He had a pointy chin, spiky blond hair and a really wide grin, although he hadn't been smiling when Mr Carson was shouting at him.

'Use mine,' Patrick said, nudging his calculator towards Sammy.

'Thanks, dude,' Sammy whispered back.

For the rest of the lesson, they took turns to use the calculator, nudging it between their elbows when they were sure Mr Carson wasn't looking. Patrick forgot all about Jake. He almost forgot about Monty too, *almost* but not quite. A large, hungry polar bear in your

garage was, after all, pretty hard to forget about.

Patrick considered telling Sammy about Monty. He really wanted to but he wasn't sure it was the right thing to do. What if Sammy got scared and told someone, and that person told the police, or the army, or expert animal trackers with guns, or whoever it was that came after being told there was a polar bear on the loose?

Patrick liked Sammy but he wasn't sure he could risk putting him, and Monty, in danger.

He wished he'd told Mr Crankly that it *was* him who made the paw print on the front lawn, that it had been a joke. Mr Crankly would have told Patrick's mum, and Patrick would have gotten into trouble, but at least Mr Crankly wouldn't suspect the print had been made by a real wild animal. Patrick hoped Mr Crankly wasn't at home right now looking up the shape and size of Monty's paw print or, even worse, sniffing around Cherry Tree Close whilst everyone else was at work or school, looking for evidence. Maybe he'd already made a plaster cast of the print like they did on *Bigfoot Hunters*.

What had Monty been doing outside the garage anyway? Patrick thought he'd better have a word with Monty about going outside, try to warn him of the trouble he could get himself into. Trouble was putting it mildly. For an educated bear, Monty certainly knew how to put himself in danger.

8

Patrick opened the garage door cautiously. Even though he was pretty sure Monty wasn't going to eat him now, his heart still beat faster than usual. He was, after all, stepping into a polar bear's den.

Monty was sitting by the bikes. His nose was buried deep in a tub of strawberry cheesecake Häagen-Dazs. It was Patrick's mum's favourite.

'I didn't know you liked ice cream,' Patrick said, taking a careful step into the garage.

'All bears have a sweet tooth,' Monty said,

sweeping his tongue around the almost empty container.

He supposed it made sense that if Winnie the Pooh liked honey, polar bears might like strawberry cheesecake Häagen-Dazs.

'It is, in actual fact, common knowledge, amongst those in the know, that polar bears are rather partial to condensed milk. I couldn't find any but I found this which I believe is also made from the milk of the female cow.'

'Condensed milk?' Patrick wasn't sure he'd ever tasted condensed milk. He'd seen a tin of it in his nan's cupboard, along with Spam, orange jelly cubes and tinned broad beans. He'd certainly never had it at home. He wondered how Monty, or any other polar bear for that matter, had discovered a taste for a food that was usually kept in the back of cupboards.

'It was a Russian explorer,' Monty explained, as if reading Patrick's mind. 'He

gave my great-grandfather, Wilbur Ambrose
Cecil Barnaby Montague the first (Willy to
his friends), a tin of condensed milk.' Monty
tossed the empty ice cream tub aside, amongst
the empty sardine tins. 'Great-Grandpa Willy
was just a cub then. He never got over the
taste of the stuff and was always talking
about it. He even wrote
a   poem   about it.'

Monty put his paw on his heart,
closed his eyes, and cleared his throat.
'O condensed milk
how I love thee!
You can keep your gold and diamonds

and your finest robes of silk
for there is no treasure finer
than a tin of condensed milk…'

Monty opened his eyes. 'Hm, I seem to have forgotten the rest of the poem. Now, of course, dear boy, *seal* remains the number one choice for dinner for *all* polar bears, but I've never known a bear pass up an opportunity to try a tin of condensed milk. It's become something of a legend amongst polar bears, thanks to old Willy.'

'I'll see if the Co-op has any,' Patrick said, shaking his head and unzipping his rucksack.

'Oh, don't mock me, dear boy.'

'No, I really will. Here, look, I've brought you some more tinned sardines.'

Patrick had bought another eight tins, almost clearing the Co-op out of sardines altogether. What would he do if they didn't replenish their stock quickly? Tesco was all the way over the other side of town and

he wouldn't be able to get there before the weekend. Even then, it would be difficult. He'd have to lie to his mum about where he was going and he hated lying. Another problem was that he didn't have much pocket money left. He'd emptied the last of his money tin now.

'Spiffing,' Monty, said, eyeing the tinned fish. 'I'm becoming rather partial to these hors d'oeuvres.'

Patrick thought hors d'oeuvres meant some kind of starter, or snack. Each tin of sardines probably was about the equivalent of an olive to Monty. Not much of a meal. Hardly a walrus, or a seal. There couldn't be much left in the chest freezer either. Maybe the condensed milk would make Monty happy. He must try to get some.

'Have you been out of the garage?' Patrick asked, thinking of the paw print on Mr Crankly's lawn.

'Only when nature called,' Monty replied.

'When nature…? Oh. I see.' Patrick looked embarrassed.

He couldn't tell Monty not to go to the bathroom. He wondered exactly where Monty had been to the bathroom but then decided he didn't want to know. Perhaps polar bear poo might be good for Mr Crankly's roses, like horse manure. Patrick was relieved anyway, to hear that Monty went *out* of the garage to go to the bathroom. The garage already smelled of bear. It wasn't unpleasant exactly, just a bit, well, *beary*.

'I'm only worried,' Patrick said slowly. 'That it might be dangerous. For you to go out, I mean.'

Monty studied Patrick carefully. 'My dear boy, the world is full of danger. If one were frightened each and every time one left the comfort of one's own abode, one would never do anything or *be* anything.' Monty cleared

his throat. 'Live life with no excuses, travel with no regret, that's what I say, although Mr Wilde said it first of course.'

Patrick frowned. 'Right… I mean, the thing is, my mum's not feeling well and I worry you might, um, startle her – if she saw you out and about, that is. Also, we've got this really mean neighbour, Mr Crankly. I'm not sure he likes polar bears much and I worry he might—'

Monty waved a paw in the air dismissively. 'Being liked is overrated. Be adored or abhorred, that's what I say. Meanness is small-mindedness. I've never stood for it.'

Patrick sighed. Monty clearly wasn't understanding the seriousness of the situation.

Patrick knew it was serious. Deadly serious. If Monty was found he would be deported, or re-homed in a zoo, or killed.

He heard his mum calling him from across the garden.

'Patrick, are you there?'

'I've got to go,' he told Monty who was busy opening his third tin of sardines with his claw.

'Same time tomorrow, old chap?'

'Yes.' Patrick sighed. He felt like he had got nowhere.

'Excellent,' Monty said, rubbing his stomach. 'Perhaps you could bring me something a little more substantial?'

9

'What were you doing in the garage?'

Patrick's mum was in the kitchen chopping an onion when Patrick came in. Patrick thought it lucky the garage wasn't attached to the house like some people's garages.

'I was just looking for a box of Lego.'

'Oh, okay.' Patrick's mum went back to the onion.

Patrick knew his mum wouldn't ask him any more questions. She'd been distracted ever since Evie-Ann had died. It was as if all his mum's thoughts were now directed inside her head, instead of outside where other people still lived.

His mum had slept a lot after she'd returned from the hospital. Patrick had tiptoed around the house. He'd turned it into a game, imagining he was a secret agent as he crept across the landing. Sometimes his mum would get up late in the morning, or even in the afternoon, have a long shower, put clothes on, then go back to bed because showering and putting clothes on had made her feel tired again.

That's what they'd called Patrick's sister, Evie-Ann. There was a small silver frame on the mantelpiece in the living room with prints of her feet. Someone at the hospital had made it for Patrick's mum and dad. They must have dipped Evie-Ann's feet in ink, or paint, and pressed them onto the paper. Patrick felt strange, sometimes, when he looked at the print. He thought his dad did

too because he'd caught his dad glancing at it then looking away, as if he didn't want to think about it.

His mum was different.

If she hadn't been in bed sleeping, she'd sat on the sofa all day doing nothing, just holding the print and the little white blanket, not much bigger than a tea towel, that Evie-Ann had been wrapped in. Patrick knew the blanket was now upstairs in his parents' bedroom. He'd seen it peeking out from under his mum's pillow.

Now, Patrick's mum was a little better than she'd been back then, but she still spent a lot of time sitting on the sofa in the living room under a blanket holding a cup of tea that had gone cold. Patrick thought she must just like holding mugs of cold tea.

'I'm making a veggie chilli,' his mum said, picking up a carrot. 'I know it's one of your favourites.'

Patrick was surprised. His mum hadn't done much cooking recently. She usually managed to make him dinner but it was mostly easy things like frozen pizza, or pasta with sauce from a jar, or one of those stir-fries that came in a bag with the vegetables already chopped. Patrick didn't mind any of these dinners, but there were some meals his mum used to make that he missed: toad in the hole, cottage pie, veggie chilli and his mum's vegetable lasagne. That was the best.

Patrick liked most foods except for beetroot which he thought tasted like earth, Brussels sprouts which he thought tasted like the bottom of his P.E. bag (not that he'd ever tasted the bottom of his P.E. bag) and the funny healthy stuff his mum ate that began with a Q that his dad always said looked like budgie seed and nobody could decide how to pronounce.

Patrick was glad his mum was making veggie chilli again. It meant that she was having a good day. Patrick would tell his dad next time he called.

Mum made veggie chilli, he imagined himself saying.

That's great, his dad would say.

Oh, and by the way, not to worry you or anything, but there's a polar bear living in the garage.

He definitely couldn't say that.

His dad had been worried enough about going away when his mum wasn't feeling well.

Patrick's dad worked as a wildlife photographer, which meant he sometimes went away on trips to photograph animals. His photographs had been in magazines and used on websites. They'd even won competitions. There was one of a stoat peeping out from behind a tree that had won an award. Patrick thought the photograph was funny. It was like the stoat was saying, *Yes? Did you want something?*

Patrick's dad wasn't always able to make enough money just photographing animals so he taught photography workshops, and sometimes took on jobs that didn't involve taking pictures of animals but other things instead, like jewellery, or smoothies.

This job was in Scotland and *did* involve animals. A rich man had bought a big house with lots of land. Patrick's dad called it an *estate*. The man wanted Patrick's dad to photograph the wildlife on his *estate* so he could hang the pictures up in his big house and show them off to people when they came over for parties, and so he could make a calendar. Patrick's dad was allowed to stay at the house whilst he was photographing the wildlife as there was no one else around. He said the house was so big he kept finding

new rooms. He'd joked that he'd never had to use the same bathroom twice.

For the last week, Patrick's dad said he had gone out every day on his own with his camera, wearing his special camouflage clothing. He was looking for deer, red squirrels, mountain hares and ptarmigans – funny-looking game birds that he said turned white in the winter so it was difficult to see them against the snow.

It sounded fun, staying in a big house like that and not having to use the same bathroom twice.

You look after your mum for me, his dad had said before he left.

Patrick had been doing his best. He'd made her breakfast most mornings, including a cup of tea and, in the evenings, he'd watched his mum's favourite TV programmes with her, even the cheesy nineties detective shows he didn't like very much. He'd unloaded the dishwasher *and* put his own clothes away after they'd come out of the dryer, even pairing up his socks which had taken ages.

Patrick knew all this would reassure his dad, but he wasn't sure he was doing the best job of looking after his mum when he knew there was a hungry, carnivorous polar bear living inside the garage. He didn't think Monty would try to eat him or his mum but then he supposed you could never really know a person, or a polar bear.

Patrick's nan had said that to Patrick once, about knowing a person. It was after his Great Uncle Ron had died and left his body to medical research. *He hated going to the doctor's*, she'd said, shaking her head. *I guess you can never really know a person.*

Patrick's mum was frightened of small dogs. It was a kind of phobia. Tommy had had a Yorkshire Terrier called Fitz and Tommy's mum used to have to make sure she put Fitz in the dining room whenever Patrick's

mum came over to collect him. If his mum was scared of a small dog she would most definitely be frightened of a large polar bear.

If Monty was discovered, Cherry Tree Close would be full of armed marksmen, and TV people with giant cameras and microphones. They'd want to interview Patrick's parents. Patrick's mum hated being the centre of attention and Patrick knew she'd be mad about being seen on TV without her hair being done. Mr Crankly would tell everyone he *knew* the Jollys were a bad sort and up to something. Maybe the armed marksmen would surround the garage and call out to Monty through a megaphone like they do in films: *You are completely surrounded. Come out with your paws above your head.* Although they wouldn't do that because they wouldn't know Monty could understand what they were saying. Probably, they'd just shoot, maybe even *through* the garage door which would mean the door would be full of bullet holes and Patrick's dad would be cross because he'd have to buy a new one.

Patrick sighed. He *had* to figure out a way to get Monty back to Greenland before his dad got home, or Mr Crankly discovered him, or the Co-op ran out of tinned sardines.

10

It was 05:33 AM and Patrick was awake in bed. He had no idea what he was doing being awake at 05:33 AM when he didn't have to get up for school until seven, a whole *hour and a half* away.

It was still dark, and cold, because the heating was on a timer and didn't come on until six forty-five.

Patrick sat up. He was wearing his favourite banana pyjamas. The pyjamas were covered in half-peeled bananas in sunglasses. They used to be glow-in-the-dark but had stopped glowing a while ago after going through the wash too many times. Probably, he was too old now for glow-in-the-dark pyjamas. It was true, he'd had them a couple of years and they *were* a little short in the leg but they were soft and familiar and, anyway, who was going to see them? Patrick still liked his banana pyjamas.

He rubbed his eyes and looked at the bright numbers on his alarm clock. He'd heard about people who woke up just before something bad was about to happen to them, like maybe right before a meteorite fell from space and crashed through the roof of their house. He looked up at the ceiling. Perhaps he'd better get out of bed.

He pushed his feet into his furry Chewbacca slippers then padded across the room to the window. He *had* been intending to look up at the sky and check for meteorites but when he pushed back the curtain he found himself looking at something else instead.

The security light was on in the garden illuminating the patio and the side of the garage. But it was down the end of the garden that Patrick noticed something strange.

At the bottom of Patrick's garden there were two apple trees. At the end of summer when the apples began to fall, Patrick's mum would pick them, or gather the unbruised ones from the ground, and make apple crumble. This year had been the first year Patrick could remember that she hadn't made any crumble, or put any apples in the garage like she usually did – wrapping them in newspaper to keep them fresh. The apples had fallen just after Evie-Ann had died and so no one had bothered to pick them up. The rotting apples had laid on the ground amongst the fallen autumn leaves.

The summer before last, Patrick's dad had bought a hammock and hung it between the two apple trees. He said it was weatherproof and that they could leave it out. Patrick's dad loved all those kind of outdoorsy gadgets. He spent a lot of time outside waiting for animals so he needed to have the right gear.

Patrick went camping with his dad every summer. It was something they did together, just the two of them. His mum didn't like camping much. She'd come with them once. Unfortunately, it had rained. She said she couldn't keep her feet clean, that there were too many bugs, and she got cross when Patrick's dad suggested she wee in a bush. Neither did she think much of the solar shower Patrick's dad rigged up in the tree near their tent. She said it was like standing under a dripping tap.

She didn't like cooking on the portable stove, and having to wait a long time for the kettle to boil. She complained that Patrick's dad kept farting in the tent because of all the beans they'd been eating. Then she announced she was taking the car and going

90

home for a bath and that she'd come back for Patrick and his dad on Saturday if they insisted on staying. That was the one and only time Patrick's mum had been camping with them. Patrick had to agree with his dad that it hadn't been much of a success.

Patrick's mum did not like 'The Wilderness' as she called it. She liked restaurants, four hob rings and hot baths. She did not like camping, mud, hiking shoes or high altitudes. She liked yoga in a warm studio, clean trainers and lots of buildings around her.

For Patrick's dad, 'The Wilderness' meant living in a tent for a week with a pair of binoculars, a telephoto lens, and plenty of tinned beans.

'The Wilderness' for Patrick's mum meant an afternoon picnic in the park, or sitting in the garden with a cup of tea.

His mum loved the hammock though. When it was sunny she liked to lie in it and read her book, although she hadn't done that last summer as she'd been too pregnant and worried she might fall out.

Patrick now stared at the hammock. It was very low to the ground and there was a huge polar bear shaped mound in it. He groaned silently then turned away from the window and left his room.

He felt his way along the dark landing then crept downstairs. He absolutely did not want to wake his mum. Although this was unlikely. She'd been taking tablets that made her sleep better. She said they made her feel fuzzy-headed in the morning. One morning she'd poured orange juice over her cereal by mistake. Another morning she'd put curry powder instead of cinnamon on top of her porridge. 'Maybe I should just give up with breakfast,' she'd said. That was when Patrick had started making it for her.

At the bottom of the stairs, Patrick grabbed

his coat from the peg rail and went into the kitchen. He swapped his Chewbacca slippers for his trainers and opened the back door.

The night was still and silent, the grass wet and dewy. It was cold, really too cold to be out in the garden at five-thirty AM in the middle of January in just his banana pyjamas and school coat.

As he approached Monty, Patrick felt nervous. What did he think he was going to say to him? *Sorry, going to have to move you on. No stopping here. No, not even if you've got a ticket or bought a coffee. This isn't a public hammock.*

Patrick could hear Monty snoring loudly. That bear would sleep anywhere. It was falling asleep on the melting iceberg that had got him into trouble in the first place.

Patrick was being as quiet as he could. His dad had always told him to respect animals and their environments although, really, this was Patrick's garden, Patrick's territory.

He could feel his heart beating. His legs felt weak. He worried Monty would wake up suddenly and attack him, perhaps forgetting who Patrick was, that Patrick was the one who brought him tinned sardines.

He looked around then reached for a large stick, an apple tree branch that had blown off the tree. He moved forward again. This time with the branch out in front of him. Not that he thought it would do much good, really. It would be liked trying to defend yourself from a sabre-toothed tiger with a Twiglet. He felt a bit silly but perhaps it was better than nothing.

Monty snored again. He twitched and rolled over, causing the hammock to almost touch the ground and muttered something in his sleep that sounded like *flabberfloodooo*.

Patrick poked Monty gently with the stick. 'Monty, wake up.'

Monty continued to snore.

'Monty!' Patrick hissed.

Monty opened one eye and looked at Patrick. 'My dear boy, whatever are you doing with that?'

Patrick looked at his branch. 'I thought you might not recognise me.'

Monty sniffed. 'Don't be ridiculous. I'd know your scent anywhere.'

Patrick was slightly offended by this. He took personal hygiene very seriously and showered every day. He fought the urge to sniff his own armpits. It was too cold to unzip his coat.

'Why are you out here?' Patrick asked.

'A change is as good as a rest,' Monty said. 'The two combined is even better.'

Patrick sighed.

'Fresh air, old sport. Freedom, books, flowers and the moon, of course. All one needs to be happy.'

Patrick shivered a little. What was Monty talking about? It sounded like he was quoting again.

'Did Mr Wilde say that too?'

'He did indeed.'

Monty rolled out of the hammock and onto the grass. He stood on his four paws and shook himself, splashing Patrick with dew.

A light came on. It was one of Mr Crankly's upstairs windows. Perhaps he'd heard them talking. Monty's voice was particularly loud and deep and carried well. He had what Patrick's dad would call 'a theatrical voice'.

The security light was still shining over the patio and, even though they were at the back of the garden, if Patrick had seen Monty in

the hammock from his window it was likely Mr Crankly would be able to see them both.

Patrick's heart was racing. He could see a shadow moving behind Mr Crankly's curtains.

'Quick,' he hissed, looking around. 'Over here!' He pointed to the bonfire his dad had built a few months ago but never burned. They'd been planning to have a fireworks party in the garden and invite a few friends over. There'd be sparklers and roast chestnuts. His dad would have lit the bonfire and let off fireworks. They'd been collecting wood and rubbish for the bonfire for months but by the time the 5th November came around Patrick's mum hadn't felt well enough. They'd cancelled the party. Patrick's mum had stayed in bed and Patrick and his dad had gone to the park and watched a firework display there instead. Patrick had been disappointed.

The fireworks were pretty good but he had wished his mum could have been with them. And he still would have preferred to have had fireworks at home. He missed his mum's roast chestnuts and the hot dogs they'd been planning on having.

Now there was the bonfire over by the back fence. It was the only thing in the garden big enough to hide Monty.

'Behind here!' Patrick whispered urgently.

Monty lumbered over and squeezed into the gap between the bonfire and the back fence. Patrick crouched down next to him. He was so close to Monty he could hear him breathing. He could smell damp wood and bear.

'What's going on?' Monty said. 'This is all jolly good fun old sport, but why the need for concealment. Polar bears have no natural predators, you know.'

'Shhh,' Patrick whispered. 'It's my

neighbour. He must have heard something. Or else, he's seen the security light. Trust me, Monty. We don't want him to see us.'

Peeping from behind the bonfire, Patrick could see the curtains at the window opening. Mr Crankly appeared. Patrick could see him, even from this distance. He was wearing red and white striped pyjamas. He stood for a moment or two, looking out across the garden. He was too far away for Patrick to see the expression on his face clearly. The curtains closed but the light remained on.

'Are we out of the woods?' Monty asked.

'I'm not sure. Let's just wait a minute and see if he turns his light off.'

As Patrick watched the light at the bedroom window, he became aware of Monty shuffling about next to him. Monty had turned himself around and was rubbing his back against the bonfire, shimmying up and down.

'An excellent back-scratcher, these twigs.'

'Monty, stop it! The whole bonfire is shaking!'

Monty stopped shimmying and settled down.

'Sorry, old chum. Didn't want to disturb your game but that was most satisfying.'

Patrick wished this was all just a game.

Mr Crankly's light went out and Patrick breathed a sigh of relief. 'All clear,' he told Monty.

'Splendid. Perhaps I will take a stroll back to the ice after all.'

At first Patrick thought Monty meant Greenland, then he realised he just meant the freezer.

'That might be best.'

Monty sloped off back to the garage, nudging the door open with his nose. Patrick watched as Monty's rear end and short stubby tail disappeared inside.

Phew.

100

That had been a close call.

Patrick quickly crossed the garden. It was so cold he could see his breath in front of his face. He didn't expect he'd get much sleep now until his alarm went off. Still, he couldn't wait to get back under his thick, warm duvet. He opened the kitchen door and was about to step inside when he noticed a fox sitting by one of his mum's plant pots. The fox looked at Patrick for a few seconds then trotted off.

'I wouldn't go near the garage if I were you,' Patrick called after it. 'Not unless you want to be a polar bear's lunch.'

11

Patrick had just drifted off back to sleep when his alarm went off. It was still dark outside. His mum used to hate going to work in the dark then coming home in the dark, although she hadn't been to work for a long time. In different circumstances he wouldn't have minded his mum being at home more but, as it was, all he wanted was for her to be better again.

Patrick's mum worked for a local magazine. She'd gone back to work full time when Patrick started school which meant his dad had picked him up – unless he was

working then his nan would collect him. Unless she was at her senior keep-fit class. In that case Patrick would go over to Tommy's house.

The magazine Patrick's mum worked for was thin and glossy and had lots of pictures inside of local restaurants and houses for sale. Patrick's mum was the editor which meant she wrote articles for the magazine and organised how it looked.

Before Patrick had been born his mum worked for a big newspaper in London. That's how his parents met. Patrick's dad (who hadn't been called Patrick's dad then but Owen) had been hired by the newspaper for a short time to take photographs to go with the news stories. He'd come into the office and Patrick's mum (who wasn't called Patrick's mum then but Jessica) offered him a coffee, only she couldn't get the new coffee machine to work. Patrick's dad, with his beard, longer hair and brown corduroy trousers, had helped her figure the machine out.

Patrick's dad said he was very nervous and that his hand was shaking a little bit when he gave her the cup of coffee. He was worried he might spill some over his new shirt.

But why were you nervous? Patrick liked to ask his dad.

His dad's answer was always the same.

Because I am always nervous around beautiful and intelligent women and your mother is the most beautiful and intelligent woman I've ever met.

It had taken Patrick's dad almost a month to ask his mum out for dinner. When he finally did, he took her for a Thai curry. He said he thought she was probably seeing someone: a politician or a film star, or a rich businessman with five yachts. Patrick's dad didn't think someone like his mum, someone beautiful and clever, would want to go out with an often out-of-work, scruffy photographer who

took pictures of families whose televisions had exploded, or kids whose gerbils had had eleven babies at once. She wouldn't want to go out with a man who liked to spend his weekends hiding in tents waiting for badgers.

It turned out Patrick's mum *had* wanted to go out with a man like Patrick's dad. In fact, she had married him.

Patrick's parents had moved to the house they lived in now when Patrick's mum had become pregnant with Patrick.

Patrick's dad had been happy because living further out of London meant they were a little bit closer to the countryside. He joked that the downside was that they were also a little bit closer, in fact quite *a lot* closer, to Patrick's nan – his mother-in-law.

Patrick's mum didn't think that was funny.

Patrick's mum always said she called Patrick 'Patrick' because she not only liked the sound of the name but because of what it meant. All names have a meaning, she liked to say – it wasn't just something they made up to make you buy a key ring from museum gift shops.

Patrick's name meant 'noble'. Patrick had once looked up the meaning of the word. It had said something about a person who had high moral principles.

Morals, Patrick knew, meant knowing right from wrong. Patrick's mum thought someone having 'high moral principles' made them a good person. She said that more than wanting Patrick to grow up to be an astronaut, or an Olympic swimmer, she wanted him to be a good person, although he could still be an astronaut or an Olympic swimmer if he wanted to.

Patrick's dad had said he liked the name because his grandmother had been Irish and Patrick is the patron saint of Ireland,

although Patrick's dad had never actually been to Ireland.

Patrick wanted to live up to his mum's expectations. He thought being noble was probably going to be a bit easier than being an astronaut. He knew a lot of kids wanted to go into space but he wasn't so sure about it himself. There was all that darkness and nothingness, all those black holes to fall into, and how did astronauts go to the loo?

As for being an Olympic swimmer, that probably wasn't going to happen either. Patrick had had swimming lessons at junior school. Once a week his class went on a coach to the local pool. You had to get your twenty-five-metre badge by the end of term or else you were made to go back the next year with another class of kids younger than you. Patrick had known he *had* to get the badge. Twenty-five metres had been a long way and he *might just* have put his foot down a couple of times when Mrs Hitchcock, the swimming teacher, hadn't been looking, but he did get his badge.

However, he would have to stick with being noble for now.

Patrick got out of bed, put his slippers on, and went over to the window. The hammock was still empty, which was good, but now there was something else to worry about.

Mr Crankly was out in his garden. He was dressed smartly, as he always was, in a shirt, tie and a green cardigan. Patrick wondered why Mr Crankly wore a shirt and tie even though he was retired. He couldn't wait to get his tie off when he got home. You weren't supposed to take your tie off on the *way home* from school because it would make you look unkempt and give the school a bad reputation, so the head teacher, Mr Plimmswood, said.

Mr Crankly, in his shirt and tie, was standing next to his pond. He was just sort of staring

108

at it. Patrick reached for his binoculars. They were very good binoculars. His dad had bought them for him for his tenth birthday. They were useful for helping his dad spot wildlife when he went out with him.

Patrick crouched down so that if Mr Crankly were to look up, he would only see the top of Patrick's head and the binoculars, which hopefully wouldn't look like much from a distance. Through the binoculars, Patrick could see that Mr Crankly was staring at his pond and frowning. He seemed to be looking for something.

'Patrick, are you up, love?'

Patrick's mum was calling him from the landing.

'Just getting ready,' Patrick called back. He put the binoculars down on the windowsill. Whatever Mr Crankly was doing out in the garden at seven AM, whatever he was looking for, Patrick didn't think it was good.

He'd have to figure it out later. Right now, he had to get ready for school. He was running late.

On the way to school Patrick sang a little tune to himself. It was one his dad liked to sing when he was unloading the dishwasher.

There's a rat in me kitchen what am I gonna do.

Only Patrick changed some of the words.

There's a polar bear in me garage what am I gonna do.

He knew his lyrics were silly but singing the song to himself cheered him up a bit.

12

Patrick sat in registration. He felt like he had this big swirling current of worry inside him and he wasn't sure how to make it go away. He thought maybe someone could stick a tube in him and drain it out like they drained the fat out of people who had liposuction – an operation to make them slim. He'd seen it on TV.

Patrick imagined all his worry being drained into a jar. Maybe his worry would be a mix of orange and blue like those bottles of coloured layered sand people bought you when they came back from holiday. Patrick imagined going to the end of a very long pier, opening the jar of worry and tipping it out into the sea. All his worry, gone. That would be nice.

Whilst the others were talking about the new FIFA game, Patrick decided he would make another list to help clear his head. He would write down, in the back of his homework diary, the things he wanted most.

Things Patrick Jolly wants:

1. Mum to be happy again.
2. Jake Sutherland to leave me alone.
3. Monty to get safely back to Greenland.

It was a short list. Not like the Christmas lists he used to make where he basically just went through the Argos catalogue and wrote down every item in the toy section until he ran out of paper. This wish list was surely much more

112

reasonable. He used to always get some of the things from his Christmas list. He hoped he would get at least some from this list too.

The bell rang for first lesson. Patrick closed his homework diary and picked up his bag.

First lesson was P.E.

After they'd changed, Patrick stood on the school field in his P.E. kit next to Sammy who was shivering.

Patrick had noticed that some of the kids had been a bit funny with him since Jake had started picking on him. When Patrick had spoken to Gavin and Arnav, two boys in his tutor group, at lunch the day before, they'd looked uncomfortable, mumbled a bit, then glanced over to where Jake, Caleb and Luke were standing as if they wanted to make sure Jake hadn't seen them talking to him.

Of course the less popular kids didn't mind Patrick hanging around with them. They weren't bothered about Jake and just looked down at their shoes whenever he passed them, but often they were hard to find at lunch time because they were busy at chess club or science club or learning coding in the I.T. room. They didn't look you in the eye much when they spoke to you so it was kind of hard to figure out if they were okay with you hanging around them or not.

At least Sammy wasn't ignoring him. He'd cracked Patrick up at lunch yesterday when he'd put two carrot sticks in his mouth like they were fangs and started talking like Mr Carson as a vampire. *Forgot your pen? Then I'll just have to eat you, you ignoramus.* (That was the word!) Patrick had then told Sammy about Jake, Luke and Caleb bumping into Mr Crankly as he stepped out of the post office, and that Mr Crankly had accused them of throwing a crisp packet in his roses. Sammy couldn't stop laughing at that. 'Ha. I wish I'd been there,' he'd said.

Today in P.E. they were playing football. The girls had gone up to the top playground for hockey. Patrick was secretly glad he didn't have to play hockey. Those sticks looked lethal. Karima Saley had been limping all last week after Hattie Crenshaw had accidentally whacked her on the ankle whilst going for the ball.

Mr Larson, their P.E. teacher, was shouting at them to quieten down.

'Jake, and Caleb, please choose your teams.'

Patrick groaned.

Mr Larson had, *of course*, chosen the meanest kid in their tutor group, plus one of his minions, to head up the two teams. Jake, Luke or Caleb were often picked to choose. Mr Larson liked them. He was probably the only teacher who did.

Patrick stood and watched as other boys were chosen before him. He saw Caleb's gaze hover over him then move across to Jake who shook his head. They were going to make sure he was picked last.

Sammy hadn't been picked either. Patrick felt bad for Sammy. He was sure Sammy hadn't been picked because the others knew they sat together a lot. Although, admittedly, Sammy was pretty rubbish at football.

They were now the last two kids standing on the field. Patrick could feel his cheeks burning. Everyone was looking at him and Sammy. It was Jake's turn to pick. He looked from Patrick to Sammy then grinned.

'Hurry up, Sutherland,' Mr Larson said. 'We haven't got all day.'

Jake pointed at Sammy and then at Patrick. 'Ip, dip, doo, old Plimmy did a poo…'

'Sutherland!'

Jake shrugged. 'I'll take Brolly then.'

Patrick moved over to where Jake's team were and Sammy went over to Caleb's.

'You'd better not lose this for us, Brolly,'

Jake whispered in Patrick's ear. 'And, by the way, you're a defender.'

Patrick shook his head. How did anyone take Jake seriously?

He didn't like being threatened, or being picked last. And Jake *knew* Patrick's best position was midfield.

It wasn't fair. Jake Sutherland might live in a big house, and look like he should be in a boy band with his sweepy hair and high cheek bones, but he was mean, and he made everyone scared of him.

Being kind, or noble, didn't seem to count for much at secondary school. There was a hierarchy, a pecking order. Jake was like a great white shark that swam right at the top of the ocean with its mouth open, eating all the fish it could find. Patrick had always thought of himself as a friendly turtle, bothering no one, but Jake had somehow reduced him to a bottom feeder, one of those weird-looking fish that ate everyone else's leftovers and buried their heads in the sand when things got too difficult.

It was true, Patrick didn't sit at the cool table at lunch, but neither was he the type of kid that got picked on, or was chosen last for sports. Not until recently, anyway. He had always liked to think of himself as somewhere in the middle. Neutral territory. Like Switzerland during the Second World War (his dad had told him about it). Yep, that was him – Friendly Turtle Switzerland. Until now.

I am not a bottom feeder, Patrick thought to himself. He shot a look at Jake who was re-tying his laces before the match started. *And I won't let you treat me like one, Jake Sutherland.*

Three minutes after kick-off, Jake tackled Tomasz Walker for the ball, knocking him to the ground. It was probably a foul but Mr

118

Larson did nothing. There were four players in front of Jake.

Patrick called for the ball. 'Pass it back!'

Jake turned and grinned at him. 'Here you go then, Brolly.' He booted the ball as hard as he could at Patrick where it hit him hard on the side of his head and bounced into the goal.

'Own goal. One nil, to Caleb's team!' Mr Larson shouted.

Jake sniggered. 'Way to go, Brolly.'

'Brolly, you wally!' Luke called out.

Patrick was mortified. Jake had made him look stupid in front of the whole class. This time Jake had really taken things too far.

13

Patrick opened the garage door. He had his rucksack on his back, full of tinned sardines (the Co-op had had a delivery) and three tins of condensed milk. He'd used the very last of his money.

He'd been saving for a day trip to London his dad had promised they'd have together when he got back from Scotland. He'd said they could go to the London Dungeons, or a VR arcade, or maybe even take a stadium tour, although that might have to be for his birthday too which was next month – the 15th February. Patrick's mum always said

she'd thought Patrick was going to be born on Valentine's Day. 'The best Valentine's present ever!' she'd told him. But he actually arrived the next day. Patrick was glad about that. He wouldn't have wanted his birthday on Valentine's Day. Other people might get more cards, and Nando's was likely to be full of couples holding hands and kissing over their chicken and fries.

Anyway, wherever they went for their day trip, Patrick knew it would be good to have a bit of spending money. That probably wouldn't be the case now. Oh, well. He didn't mind using his money on Monty, he just didn't know what he was going to do tomorrow now that it had run out.

Monty was awake. He had pulled down the box of Patrick's dad's camera equipment and was rummaging through it. There were a couple of old cameras in the box, along with a mini-tripod and a bag. Monty was fiddling with one of the cameras. He seemed to be having a bit of trouble holding it in his paws.

'Erm. Those are my dad's,' Patrick said, stepping into the garage and closing the door behind him. 'They're quite expensive… He'll go nuts if you break them. I can teach you how to take a photograph though, if you like.'

Monty looked up at Patrick with an expression of horror. 'My dear boy, a bear like me was born to be *in front* of the camera. Certainly not *behind it*.'

'Oh, sorry.'

Monty turned to Patrick, straightening himself up. 'The Montagues have a long history of fame. There was Great Uncle Willy of course. He was photographed enjoying a tin of condensed milk given to him by a Russian explorer.'

'Yes, you mentioned—'

'And then there was my father's cousin, Cecil Montague. He was a star back in the

early nineties. Featured both in *National Geographic*, and then in a three-part feature documentary, *Secrets of the Artic*. Yes, indeed, Cecil was quite the celeb, until the incident with the baby seal. It really isn't the fault of a polar bear if you humans find our lunch 'cute'.

Patrick winced. 'Actually, speaking of condensed milk – I've brought you some.'

Monty put the camera down. 'Oh, don't tease me.'

'No, I really have.' Patrick reached into his rucksack for the tins.

Monty gasped. He picked up one of the tins and looked at it. He hooked a claw into the ring-pull and peeled back the lid. He put his nose, and tongue, straight into the tin and slurped noisily. When he was done he sat back and sighed, closing his eyes. 'Delicious. Willy was right. That, old chap, was pure ambrosia. Food of the gods, dear boy.' Monty opened his eyes and reached for the second tin. 'This is the life,' he said, leaning back against the chest freezer. 'We don't need much to be happy. The stars, good memories, and a tin of condensed milk.'

'Um, yes,' Patrick said.

It was then he noticed the fish tails on the garage floor. There were four of them. They were mostly white but one of them was a little bit orange.

'Monty, where did those fish tails come from?'

'Ah. Those fish tails were once attached to a particular Japanese delicacy.'

Patrick frowned. 'Yes, but where did you get them?'

Monty waved a paw in the air. 'From the seal hole over the boundary. So very convenient. I settled myself down to wait for a young pup to come up for a breath of air but none materialised so I decided to sample the available sashimi.'

Patrick rubbed his head with his hand. 'That isn't a seal hole. That's Mr Crankly's pond.'

'Difficult to tell the difference,' Monty said. 'It looked very much like a seal hole to me. Not much between them really.'

Patrick inhaled deeply. He looked at the fish tails again. So that's what Mr Crankly was doing out in his garden, staring at his pond this morning. He was wondering where his koi carp had gone.

'It is part of the wonderful experience of travel,' Monty said. 'That one gets to sample new cuisine. Travel improves both the mind and the palate.'

'But you weren't intending to travel anywhere,' Patrick reminded Monty. 'You drifted on a piece of broken ice until it melted under your bum and you fell into the North Sea.'

'One must take one's opportunities, dear

boy. There is often a silver lining to an unintended cloud.'

Patrick took the tinned sardines from his bag and put them next to the freezer. He shook his head. An unintended cloud? Was that all Monty thought of the situation? Monty had been here too long now. And each time he left the garage, he put his life at risk.

'There is nothing like travel,' Monty continued. 'A little refreshment for the soul, old chap.' He cleared his throat. 'A man of ordinary talent will always be ordinary, whether he travels or not; but a man of superior talent will go to pieces if he remains forever in the same place.'

'Is that Mr Wilde?' Patrick asked, wearily.

'No,' Monty said. 'I believe it was the great composer, Wolfgang Amadeus Mozart.'

Patrick sighed. Monty was always coming out with this kind of stuff. Maybe there was something in it, although he wasn't sure a

garage full of junk in Hertfordshire was really much of a 'silver lining'.

Monty really didn't seem at all worried about anything.

Patrick thought of his own 'cloud', the trouble he was having with Jake Sutherland at school. There didn't seem to be much of a silver lining to that either. He wondered how Monty would deal with Jake Sutherland. Probably, he'd just eat him.

'That Japanese delicacy you sampled. The sushi, I mean.'

'Sashimi,' Monty corrected him.

'Sashimi. They were Mr Crankly's koi carp. I think he was probably quite fond of them.' Patrick tried to be as diplomatic as he could. He didn't want Monty getting angry with him for telling him what he could and couldn't eat.

'There's no use in feeling attached to one's lunch,' Monty said, looking Patrick squarely in the eye. 'Mother Nature, dear boy, is red in tooth and claw.'

Patrick gulped. He *had* hoped Monty was growing attached to *him*, and that *he* would never be a possibility for Monty's lunch. Perhaps Monty didn't think that way.

'Anyway,' Monty said, rubbing a paw over his belly. 'You can always blame it on the heron. I've seen the way he looks at those fish. He's a crafty fellow, that one. Goes by the name of Frank. Listens to punk rock. I wouldn't put much past him.'

Patrick picked up his rucksack. It was all so confusing. Talking ducks, herons called Frank. He couldn't think clearly about the situation when Monty was talking to him.

'Aren't you going to stick around for a bit, old chap? I found a stack of board games on the top shelf. Thought we could have a go at Scrabble.'

'Sorry,' Patrick said, shaking his head. 'I

can't be here long. Mum will wonder what I'm doing. I've got homework to do.'

This *was* true. Patrick couldn't let his homework slip. If he got detention he'd be late feeding Monty. His mum might start asking questions as to why he wasn't doing his homework. He couldn't tell her it was because he was busy talking to a polar bear about travel and herons. And what if he was grounded. How would he get to the Co-op?

'Ah,' said Monty. 'Yes, schoolwork *must* come first. Mark my words, old chap; a man of education, integrity, character, and a little grit between his teeth can take on the world.'

'Who said that then?' Patrick asked.

'I did,' Monty said, looking pleased with himself.

14

Patrick checked everywhere. Trouser pockets, coat pockets, under the bed and down the back of the sofa.

70p.

That definitely wasn't enough to feed a polar bear. The situation was getting desperate.

He went downstairs and into the kitchen. Under the sink, he found the grey bucket, a large sponge and a yellow cloth. He filled the bucket with warm water, added a squirt of washing up liquid then put his trainers on

and went out into Cherry Tree Close. It was still light and luckily not raining.

He tried Simon and Simon first but there was no answer, only a bark from Rudolph. Mr and Mrs Abidi weren't in either, only Sanaya, who wasn't sure if the car needed washing or not. He crossed the road to the Wilkinsons'.

Mrs Wilkinson opened the door in her dressing gown. She was wearing a pink shower cap and she had a bright green face.

'Hello, Patrick.'

Patrick stepped back, slightly alarmed.

'Oh, sorry, did I startle you?' Mrs Wilkinson pointed to her face. It's seaweed and spearmint. It's supposed to be invigorating and rejuvenating. To be honest, it's a bit tingly… What can I do you for?' Mrs Wilkinson's eyes peered down at Patrick. She looked very strange. Even her eyebrows were green.

Patrick held up his bucket. 'I'm running a car-washing service. Five pounds for a wash and polish. Tonight only,' he added. 'Special offer.'

Mrs Wilkinson smiled. 'Well aren't you industrious.' She looked over at her large silver four by four parked on the drive. 'Go on then. You can do the Toyota if you like. Do you need paying in advance?'

'Um, yes,' Patrick said, although he hadn't thought that far ahead.

'Hang on just a minute then.'

Mrs Wilkinson disappeared into the house. When she came back she gave Patrick a five pound note which he slipped into his jeans pocket.

Then he was left alone to wash the car.

Patrick had been planning to knock on every door in Cherry Tree Close and wash as many cars as he could, but washing the Wilkinsons' car took so long he decided one

car was enough for the evening. He'd at least be able to get some more food for Monty tomorrow. Besides, it was beginning to get dark.

When he returned to the house, forty-five minutes later, tired and damp, his mum was sitting at the table staring at a cup of tea.

Patrick emptied the dirty water into the sink.

'What have you been doing with that bucket?' his mum asked.

'I washed the Wilkinsons' car for five pounds.'

Patrick's mum looked confused.

'It's entrepreneurial week at school,' Patrick said, quickly. 'We have to find jobs to do.' It was a necessary lie, he told himself, as he rinsed out the bucket.

'You could have done the hoovering here for a pound,' his mum said, helpfully.

A pound wouldn't get Monty much fish. He also *really* didn't like hoovering.

'It has to be outside the house,' he said hastily.

'Oh, I see.' His mum looked back at her screen.

It was then Patrick noticed Monty. He was in the garden weeing against the fence. The kitchen window was right behind Patrick's mum.

Patrick froze, his hand on the cupboard door. He opened his mouth then quickly closed it again and forced himself to put the bucket in the cupboard, all the time keeping an eye on Monty. *Act normally*, he told himself. He realised his hand was shaky and his chest felt tight from where he'd forgotten to breathe.

Monty finished his wee, washed his paws in the bird bath, then headed back down the garden to the garage. Unfortunately, Monty

saw Patrick standing in the kitchen. He stopped at the window and waved a paw.

His mum looked up again. 'It's good they get to do these things,' she was saying. 'Use your initiative.'

'Yes,' Patrick replied. 'It's, um, confidence building.' He jerked his head to the left, trying to tell Monty to go back inside the garage. If his mum turned around she'd see Monty standing behind her at the window waving a paw in the air which, although supposed to be friendly, might look quite threatening.

Patrick jerked his head again. *Go away! Get back in the garage!*

'Are you okay?' his mum asked.

'Just stretching,' Patrick said.

'It looks uncomfortable.'

'I might have pulled something washing Mrs Wilkinson's car. We did yoga today in P.E. It's a new pose. I thought it might help.' Patrick tried to stretch his neck out to the left a little more. He lifted his right leg off the ground. 'It's called, um, wandering bear.'

Monty was now pressing his nose against the glass, causing it to steam.

'I've never heard of that one,' Patrick's mum said. She sighed. 'This tea has gone cold. I'll make a fresh one.'

Patrick lifted his left arm and pointed slowly and steadily in the direction of the garage.

Monty finally got the message. He lumbered back into the garage just as Patrick's mum stood and turned towards the window and the kettle.

Patrick let out a sigh of relief.

'That really is a very strange pose,' his mum said, glancing back at him. 'At least you're remembering to breathe.'

15

Thursday morning was bin day.

As Patrick set off for school, he could see that the bin men hadn't been yet, not only because the bins were all out but because there was rubbish all over Cherry Tree Close. Some of the bins had been knocked over. Black bags were spewing their contents onto the pavements.

It was a bright and sunny morning, although still cold. A few of Patrick's neighbours were standing next to the bins scratching their heads or righting the bins that had fallen over. Mrs Wilkinson was out in her dressing

gown and a pair of pink slippers with cat faces on them. She was picking up rubbish with one of those long sticks that had pincers on the end.

The only bins that hadn't been knocked over were those belonging to Patrick's house. Patrick was glad about this because the recycling bin was full of the empty sardine tins he'd gathered up from the garage floor and rinsed out himself. A whole wheelie bin full of sardine tins was bound to look suspicious.

As he stood at the end of the drive, he heard a noise behind him. The noise was somewhere between a growl and a hiss. He turned and saw Mr Crankly standing at the end of his own driveway. He was glaring at Patrick.

Patrick swallowed and tried to move away but it was too late: Mrs Wilkinson was striding towards them in her cat slippers.

'Well, I don't know,' she said, shaking her

head. 'Geoffrey says it must have been a fox. He's been through every bin except the Jollys'. It must have got spooked. What a mess!'

Mr Crankly made the hissing growling noise again. 'It's no fox,' he said, his eyes narrowing. 'This is the work of a much larger animal. A true predator.'

Mrs Wilkinson looked alarmed. 'What do you mean? It must be a fox. There aren't any larger animals. I mean, you hear about things escaping, don't you, but if anything had escaped, from the zoo or one of the wildlife parks, I'd have heard about it. I always listen to the local radio in the morning whilst doing the dishes and I didn't hear anything of the sort.'

Patrick had been pretending to study his shoes. He could feel Mr Crankly's eyes on him.

'There's something out there,' Mr Crankly said, looking towards the trees at the back of

Cherry Tree Close, 'and I intend to find out what it is.'

With that, Mr Crankly turned and went back inside his house.

Mrs Wilkinson sighed. 'I wouldn't worry about him, dear. He's always been a little on the grouchy side. Especially since Susan died. You did a great job on the car last night. How's your mum, love?'

'She's okay,' Patrick said, not wanting to tell Mrs Wilkinson that his mum was still taking tablets to sleep and sitting on the sofa in the middle of the day holding mugs of cold tea.

'Good,' Mrs Wilkinson said. 'You let us know if you need anything.'

'Thanks. I had better get to school.'

'You run along, love. And don't worry about old grouchy pants over there.' She nodded in the direction of Mr Crankly's front door. 'He's letting his imagination run away with him. That's all.'

'Okay,' Patrick said, wishing this were true.

'Give my regards to your mum.'

Patrick said that he would.

As he walked away, he wondered how Mrs Wilkinson might feel if she'd known that, as she was talking to Patrick at the end of his drive, she'd been standing only a few metres away from a large carnivorous polar bear asleep in the chest freezer in his garage.

There were some things, he decided, that people were better off never knowing.

16

Patrick was walking out of the science classroom with Sammy when he saw Jake, Caleb and Luke hanging around in the corridor.

Patrick and Sammy were the last ones out of the room as Sammy had lost his pencil sharpener under the Bunsen burner cupboard and they'd had to get down on their hands and knees after the bell had gone and flick it out with a ruler.

It was break time and most of the others had gone to their lockers already. The corridor, apart from Jake, Luke and Caleb, was empty.

Jake stood there grinning at them.

'Got any fish in your bag today, Brolly?' Luke asked.

Jake and Caleb laughed.

Sammy looked confused.

'Yeah,' Jake said. 'We reckon you're secretly half fish, Brolly. Like a mermaid. Maybe your whole family are mermaids.' Jake prodded Patrick in the ribs with his elbow. 'Bet you're all covered in scales under there.'

'Bet Sammy's one too,' Caleb said, helpfully.

'Yeah. A pair of mermaids,' Jake said.

Patrick had intended to walk past Jake without saying anything, without responding to his stupid primary school comments. He couldn't believe it when he found himself turning towards Jake. It was probably because Jake had mentioned his family, and because he was being nasty to Sammy. It was one thing to be mean to Patrick for no reason but

144

it wasn't okay for Jake to start bringing other people into it.

'Shut up,' Patrick said. 'Just shut up.'

'You've done it now,' Luke said to Jake. 'Brolly's mad.'

Patrick looked down at his fists. He hadn't realised he was clenching them. This time he wasn't going to let Jake get away with teasing him. This time he was going to stand up for himself.

'Nobody cares what you think, Jake Sutherland because you're *nobody*. You think you're great but you're not. Nobody cares about your lame jokes. I could have come up with something better than that when I was *seven*. Everyone else has better things to do with their lives, everyone except *you*. I'm surprised you even know what a mermaid is, seeing as your imagination, like your brain, is the size of a *pea*.'

Whilst Patrick had been saying all this

he'd been edging further and further away from Jake, Caleb and Luke. Sammy had also been stepping back along with him. They were actually quite far along the corridor now which was a good thing as Jake had a funny expression on his face.

It was an expression that was somewhere between shock and disbelief. It seemed to say: *Are you actually talking to me like that? Me? Jake, the great white shark? King of the Ocean? Most popular Year Seven boy at Priestwood Comprehensive?*

After Patrick had stopped talking there was a tiny pause before Jake recovered from his shock. 'Get him,' he hissed.

'Run!' Sammy shouted, and then they were running along the corridor with Jake, Luke and Caleb chasing them. They ran past the science classrooms on the third floor then down the stairs to the second floor. Jake, Luke and Caleb were still chasing them. They

could hear their footsteps coming down the stairs.

'We've got you, Brolly!' Jake was shouting.

Patrick and Sammy raced along the humanities corridor then turned a corner, Sammy skidding on the shiny floor. As they ran past a closed door with a sign on it saying STAFFROOM, Sammy pounded on the door with his fists.

They turned another corner and found themselves at the top of the staircase.

Sammy grabbed Patrick and pulled him behind some lockers.

They heard shouting and yelping, and then a smashing sound.

'Argghhhhhh.'

Patrick and Sammy crept out from behind the lockers.

There was Mr Plimmswood, getting up off the floor, red in the face. He was holding half an egg and cress sandwich. The other half was stuck to his jacket. He had a smear of egg on his tie. His mug that said *Top Teacher* on it had broken, spilling tea all over the corridor floor.

Jake, Luke and Caleb were in a pile, a tangle of arms, legs and blazers.

Mr Plimmswood must have opened the staffroom door just as Jake, Caleb and Luke had run past. Jake had run straight into Mr Plimmswood and Luke and Caleb had run straight into Jake.

Sammy had his hand over his mouth to stop himself from laughing.

'My favourite mug!' Mr Plimmswood bellowed.

Jake, Luke and Caleb were struggling to untangle themselves and get to their feet.

'Sorry, sir,' Jake muttered.

Mr Plimmswood was so angry, Patrick thought he could almost see the steam coming out of his ears. 'That mug was a Christmas present from Mrs Plimmswood!' He looked

at the pieces of his mug on the floor then pulled a handkerchief from his pocket and dabbed at the egg on his jacket. 'I've got a meeting with the governors this afternoon and I haven't got a spare jacket. You knocked me clean off my feet. Detention tonight for all three of you! Running in the corridors – anyone would think you're still at primary school. And don't you think I don't know who you are.' Mr Plimmswood glared at Jake. 'Not only will I be writing to your parents, Sutherland, but I'll be informing Mr Larson to drop you from the team for Thursday's match against Sanderson School.'

'But sir…'

'Enough! I shall see you *all* at four fifteen. My office.'

Mr Plimmswood marched off along the corridor. He passed Patrick and Sammy without acknowledging them and headed down the stairs.

Jake, Caleb and Luke looked around whilst Patrick and Sammy held their breath. The three boys slunk off in the direction they had come from.

Once the coast was clear, Patrick and Sammy started jumping around.

'Awesome!' Patrick said, high-fiving Sammy. 'I can't believe you thought to do that.'

Sammy grinned. 'Yeah, that was pretty quick thinking for me. I remembered what you said about your neighbour coming out of the post office.'

'Did you see the look on Jake's face? He went all pink. He nearly cried!'

'Yeah, I know. And did you see old Plimmy? He looked like he wanted to pick them up and shake them. He was so mad. "That mug was a Christmas present,"' Sammy said, blowing his cheeks out and doing a good impression of Mr Plimmswood.

'He's going to make them write lines tonight,' Patrick said. 'I heard he always makes students write lines, and he stays with them so they can't talk.'

'I heard that too,' Sammy said.

'Ha. We really showed them.'

'Yeah.' Sammy grinned. 'It was teamwork.'

They high-fived again just as the bell started ringing.

Patrick looked at his watch. 'We missed break time.'

'It was worth it though,' Sammy said. '*Totally* worth it. We just outsmarted the meanest kids in the whole year. I can't believe what you said about his brain being the size of a pea.' Sammy chuckled to himself.

Patrick smiled. 'Yeah,' he said. 'That felt good.'

17

It was helpful that Jake, Caleb and Luke had detention after school as it meant there was no way Patrick would bump into them in the Co-op.

It was also a good thing he'd earned that five pounds last night.

He tried to buy his sardines from a different check-out person each time so that he didn't become known as 'fish boy' and so no one would get suspicious.

Today he bought a tin of tuna along with the sardines. He made sure he bought the ring-pull ones so Monty could open them.

Patrick wasn't sure how good polar bears were with tin openers. It probably wasn't worth the risk. He wasn't sure what he'd do if Monty got injured. It wasn't like he could call the RSPCA.

As Patrick was on his way out of the Co-op he saw Lily Sutherland coming in.

Lily was one of those people everyone liked. She had a smile that made you feel a little bit fuzzy inside when it was directed towards you. Patrick always blushed whenever Lily smiled at him. He didn't know how mean Jake Sutherland could have such a nice sister. They were so different; like chalk and cheese, his mum would say.

Lily was looking at a piece of paper and talking to herself. It was unusual to see Lily Sutherland on her own. She had so many friends; she was usually surrounded by them, like a queen bee, or maybe more of a princess bee because didn't the queen just lie around all day laying eggs? Lily wasn't a lying-around-all-day kind of person. She was more of a get-up-and-do-something sort.

Patrick remembered how, when Lily had been at Junior School, she'd volunteered to organise the charity cake sale. She'd made flyers and told everyone to keep a list of ingredients next to their cakes in case there were any kids with food allergies. That was the sort of person Lily was: organised, thoughtful. She'd won the Junior Caring Cup two years in a row.

Patrick put his head down and pretended he hadn't seen Lily. It wasn't that he didn't like her, or didn't want to talk to her, it was just that she was *so* nice, he found it hard to know what to say. She had a sort of sparkle that made you feel lucky to be anywhere close to her. It made him nervous. He wondered if he had inherited this trait from his dad.

154

I am always nervous around beautiful and intelligent women.

It was too late.

'Patrick, hey!' Lily was smiling at him.

'Oh, hey, Lily.' Patrick smiled back. He couldn't help himself. Lily's smile was catching, like a yawn.

'I haven't seen you around much lately,' Lily said, as if they were actual friends and not just people who lived one street away from each other who were in different year groups. 'How do you like secondary school?'

'Yeah, it's okay,' Patrick said.

'I think it gets better,' Lily said, studying him carefully. 'Maybe when you're in Year Ten or something.'

Patrick couldn't imagine being in Year Ten. There were some boys in Year Ten who'd actually started shaving.

'Kids are so silly in Lower School,' Lily

said. 'It's like they're all malfunctioning or something.'

Patrick smiled. 'Yep. But you're still there?'

Lily laughed. 'Don't I know it. Year Nine is the worst, especially if you're a girl. The girls get super mean in Year Nine.'

'I'm sorry,' Patrick said. He didn't like the thought of anyone being mean to Lily.

Lily shrugged. 'That's okay. They mostly leave me alone but I've seen some nastiness go on.'

Patrick nodded. He could imagine. Girls were the worst.

Patrick wondered if Lily knew how mean her younger brother had become. He thought she probably didn't. Well, he wasn't going to be the one to tell her. She might not like it. She might think Patrick was just telling tales.

'What's that?' he asked instead, pointing

156

to all the stapled sheets of paper Lily was holding.

'It's a script for the spring show. We're doing *Beauty and the Beast*. I'm playing Belle.'

'That's great,' Patrick said, impressed.

'How's your mum?' Lily asked.

This was typical of Lily. She was so modest. She was always thinking of other people.

Patrick paused. 'She's not that good, really,' he said, wondering why he was telling Lily this. Patrick knew Lily had heard about his baby sister dying. Most people knew. A lot of them had sent sympathy cards.

'I'm sure she'll be better soon.'

'Thanks.' Patrick felt a lump rise in his throat as he said this, as if some of the sadness he felt inside was trying to escape. He swallowed it back down.

Patrick's dad was always telling him that if a man needed to cry he should cry. He said that if a person didn't cry it meant that all their feelings got squashed up inside them and made them muddled in their heads. Patrick thought his dad was probably right but, still, he didn't want to cry in front of Lily.

'Things aren't that great with my parents right now,' Lily said, glancing at her shoes. She tightened her grip on her school bag. 'Actually they're separating. Dad's sleeping on the bottom bunk in Jake's room. We're going to be moving house. Not far, but we have to move because it'll just be me, Mum and Jake.'

Patrick stared at Lily. He couldn't believe the Sutherlands were separating. They'd lived one street away from Patrick for as long as he could remember.

'I'm so sorry, Lily.'

'It's okay,' Lily said bravely. 'I think it's better. I mean – I think they'll be happier living apart. They've been kind of down

158

around each other for ages. They say they'll always be friends because of me and Jake.'

Patrick nodded. 'That's good,' was all he could think to say.

'I feel okay about it. I mean – not great – obviously. But Jake's taking it really badly. He gets angry and stuff.'

Patrick thought of Jake sitting in detention in Mr Plimmswood's office and felt kind of guilty for a moment before he remembered Jake tripping him up in the mud the other day, and then, today, Jake prodding him with his elbow to see if he was covered in scales. Then he felt not so bad.

'You must really miss Tommy,' Lily said, brushing a strand of hair away from her eyes. 'You guys used to be such good friends.'

'Yeah. I guess I do kinda miss him.'

'I remember when you did the Junior Talent Show together and you pretended to be bad magicians. That was so funny.'

'You remember that?' Patrick asked, surprised.

'Sure.'

'Actually, we weren't trying to be bad magicians. That part just sort of happened on its own.'

Lily laughed. 'I'd better go,' she said. 'I just wanted to say hi. And tell your mum I said hi.'

'I will,' Patrick said.

He watched Lily walk into the Co-op. She stopped to pick up a basket. Everything she did, she did it gracefully, like she was floating around on a little cloud or something. Patrick sighed. He hoped Lily wasn't too sad about her parents, and that she really did think it was for the best. If there was one person who deserved to always be happy, it was Lily Sutherland.

Patrick turned into Cherry Tree Close and smiled to himself, remembering Mr

Plimmswood wiping egg and cress sandwich from his suit jacket. What with that and talking to Lily, it hadn't been a bad day, all things considered.

18

When Patrick got home, he called out, as he always did, 'Mum. I'm home.'

There was no response. Patrick took his shoes off and went into the kitchen. There was a pile of washing up in the sink, their breakfast things and several mugs.

He went into the living room. The blanket was on the sofa, and some of the cushions were on the floor but his mum wasn't there.

He noticed a mug on the coffee table with a herbal tea bag in it. The tea bag was stuck to the edge of the mug, cold and shrivelled. The TV was on but there was no sound. A

man with a big moustache was holding some sort of antique bowl and pointing at it.

Patrick's mum would sit in front of the TV all afternoon watching things that Patrick knew she didn't really care about. She said she had to have the TV on because the house was too quiet without it. She couldn't read books because she couldn't concentrate on them, and she couldn't read magazines because they reminded her of work: that she should be at work, and the reason she wasn't.

Patrick turned the TV off and picked up the cushions. He looked at Evie-Ann's footprints on the mantelpiece. If only she'd lived. His mum would be busy looking after her now.

Next to the frame of Evie-Ann's footprints there was a smaller framed photograph of Patrick's mum and dad. They were on holiday, before Patrick was born, on a beach somewhere. Patrick couldn't remember where, exactly, although his mum had told him. It was one of those islands beginning with M, Minorca, Mallorca, Majorca? Patrick's dad was standing in the sea in his blue swimming shorts which he still had and Patrick's mum was wearing a pink swimming costume. Patrick's dad had lifted Patrick's mum out of the water. She was laughing and he was grinning like he'd just caught the best fish in the world. Apparently, they'd asked the ice-cream seller to take their picture. The photograph had been on the mantelpiece for as long as Patrick could remember. It was kind of embarrassing really, to have a photograph of your parents semi-naked on the living room mantelpiece.

Patrick's parents had always been like that: lovey-dovey. They liked to snuggle up against each other in the evenings and read their books or watch TV. If they were at opposite ends of the sofa, Patrick's dad would rub his mum's feet. Sometimes, after dinner,

or if they had been sitting in the living room working separately on their laptops for a while, Patrick's dad would close his Mac, take his glasses off, look over at Patrick's mum and say, *is it cuddle o'clock?* Patrick's mum would close her own laptop and say, *definitely!* They'd squish up together on the sofa and have a cuddle.

When Patrick was very small he'd joined in with *cuddle o'clock*. Of course, now, he just rolled his eyes and shook his head and wished his parents didn't have to be so embarrassing as to have things like *cuddle o' clock*.

But deep down he actually liked the fact that his parents were all lovey-dovey. He'd rather they be like that than be any other way.

That was until Evie-Ann had died.

Patrick knew his dad didn't like going away for work and being apart from them. He could tell by the way his parents kept smiling at each other when his dad returned home that they'd really missed each other.

This time was different.

Patrick had a horrible feeling – one of those feelings you don't really want to think about because you wish *so much* that it wasn't true, but one that you really can't ignore.

The feeling Patrick had was that his dad had *actually wanted* to go away this time. Things had been so difficult at home with Patrick's mum being sad and her not getting out of bed or going out much.

He knew his dad had taken the job on the country estate in Scotland because the money was good, but he also knew that wasn't the *only* reason he'd gone away.

He'd wanted to get away from all the sadness. He'd wanted to get away from Patrick's mum.

Patrick wished he could be wrong about this but he knew he wasn't.

He felt so sorry for Lily, even though she thought her parents separating was for the best. He wouldn't want his parents to be 'down around each other' as Lily had put it. He'd always want them to be happy.

Patrick knew there were a lot of things that kids didn't understand about grown-ups, that they could be complicated. It wasn't like 'going out' with a girl in Year Seven where you just had to hold the girl's hand for a while at break time, or a boy's hand of course, until, usually after a couple of weeks or so, one or the other of you would break it off, often by telling the other person's best friend that you no longer wanted to 'go out' with her or him.

Grown-up relationships were much more complicated.

Patrick liked to think that if his parents didn't want to be together anymore that he would be as grown-up and strong about it as Lily was being, although only *after* he'd had a good cry under his duvet with Mr Nutkins of course.

The thing was, Patrick was sure that deep down, under their sadness, his parents still had all those lovey-dovey feelings for each other. They were the same people as those in the photograph on the mantelpiece. Apart from the fact that his dad had less hair on the top of his head and more grey in his beard, and his mum... Well, Patrick's dad said it was impolite to say anything about a woman's age or appearance unless it was a compliment, so he'd better just leave that one right there, although, really, Patrick's mum did look mostly the same, just a little more, well, *like Patrick's mum*.

Patrick went into the kitchen to make his mum a cup of tea.

As he filled the kettle, he hoped his dad wasn't up in Scotland wishing right now that he could stay in the big house with all the bathrooms in the middle of nowhere forever.

19

Patrick always felt a little bit weird about going into his parents' bedroom, especially since his mum no longer opened the curtains. He felt like it was her place and that maybe she didn't want him there.

He slowly opened the door. The curtains were drawn and there were a lot of clothes on the floor that probably shouldn't be on the floor. There was a glass of water and a mug on his mum's bedside table.

'Mum?'

Patrick's mum was curled up in bed. She stirred then opened her eyes.

'Are you home already, Patrick?'

'Yes, it's half four.' He checked his watch. 'Actually, almost quarter to five.'

Patrick's mum smiled weakly. She sat up. 'Gosh, I only meant to sleep for half an hour. Oh, thank you,' she said, noticing the cup of tea he was holding.

Patrick put the cup of tea down on his mum's bedside table next to the other, half-drunk, one.

'I'll just have this then I'll get up,' his mum said, reaching for the fresh cup of tea.

'Okay.'

Patrick's mum used to say this a lot but most of the time she'd drink the tea then go back to sleep. She'd been a little better recently, especially around this time in the evening, because she'd want to make them both dinner. Although last Thursday when she hadn't got up, Patrick had made his own dinner – a bowl of dry cereal (because there

was no milk) and strawberry jam on crackers (because there was no bread), followed by a scoop of Häagen-Dazs ice-cream from the garage (which Monty had now eaten).

'There's no rush,' Patrick added, remembering that he had to feed Monty.

'Thank you, love.'

Patrick left his mum to drink her tea and hopefully get up.

Downstairs, he took his rucksack into the kitchen, opened the back door and slipped quietly outside.

When Patrick reached the garage door, he almost knocked. How silly, he thought, that he should have to knock to enter his own garage just because an uninvited, large, endangered animal with no natural predators had taken up residency.

Perhaps, Patrick thought, these were all very good reasons *to* knock.

He knocked.

'Enter,' Monty said, in a loud booming voice.

Patrick opened the door to find Monty lying in the freezer reading *The Complete Works of William Shakespeare.*

He had forgotten about the crate of old books and CDs that were in the garage. His dad had been meaning to take them to the charity shop for ages.

Monty placed a tinned-tuna label in the book, using it as a bookmark.

'Excellent timing. I was beginning to feel a little peckish.'

Patrick opened his rucksack and put the tuna, sardines and two tins of condensed milk on the floor.

'I saw you went out last night.'

'Only for a little nosy around. I found one or two tasty morsels.'

'Yes,' Patrick said, thinking of the overturned bins. 'Only I think Mr Crankly

172

might be getting suspicious. Especially after you ate his fish.'

Monty looked hurt. 'Fish, dear boy, cannot *belong* to anyone, despite the walruses' protests. They do become rather protective of the Arctic cod on their patch… Until they see a polar bear that is.' Monty chuckled to himself. 'It's all first come first served if you ask me.'

'The thing is,' Patrick said. 'People around here keep animals as pets. They become quite fond of them.'

'Ah, yes,' Monty said scratching his chin with his claw. 'Pets. A pampered lot if you ask me.'

'Well, I was just wondering,' Patrick said. 'If you come across any – if you'd mind not eating them.'

'Oh, I can assure you, I have very little interest in that sour-faced feline.'

'Who?'

'That furry little wretch in the red collar.'

Patrick frowned. 'That's Tinkerbell. The Wilkinsons' cat.'

'She has anger issues, if you ask me. And an obvious lack of social skills.' Monty tutted. He reached for one of the sardine tins, opened it and stuck his tongue in. He swallowed then tossed the tin over his shoulder.

'I did manage, however, to converse a little with that funny-looking wolf named after a rather implausible festive legend. Ninth in line, I reminded him, when he yapped at me from the living room window yesterday evening.'

Patrick zipped up his rucksack. 'That's Rudolph. Simon and Simon's dachshund. He's a dog.'

Monty shook his head. 'Not the brightest of mammals. But then you can't expect much from the first animal to ever be domesticated, can you?'

'I guess not,' Patrick said.

174

'Bears,' Monty said proudly, 'have *never* been domesticated.'

'Has no one ever had a pet bear?' Patrick asked.

'Well, yes, of course,' Monty said. 'But it isn't the same thing. Lord Byron kept a pet bear. Well, more of a companion really. A possible distant brown bear cousin of Uncle Cecil's, in fact. But Lord Byron was a rather fine poet so I suppose he can *almost* be forgiven.'

'Well…' Patrick said. 'I just wanted to make sure you weren't going to eat any pets, or humans of course,' he added, watching Monty carefully.

Monty shook his head. 'Polar bears don't often eat humans.'

'But they do sometimes,' Patrick said, sadly.

Monty considered this. 'Well, yes. *Sometimes.* Although it is frowned upon, in certain circles. Most bears only eat humans when either particularly hungry or particularly cranky. The problem is that polar bears nowadays are, more than often, particularly hungry or particularly cranky.'

'Oh,' Patrick said, feeling a little nervous. He took a step back. 'Why's that?' he asked, fearing the answer.

Monty sighed. 'Well, I couldn't say for sure but there seems to be an awful lot fewer seals around these days. And not just seals. Narwhals, bowheads, walruses. They all appear to be on a long vacation. It's most infuriating.'

'I don't think they're on vacation.'

He thought about telling Monty about the sixth mass extinction and that he had googled 'how endangered are polar bears' and found Monty to be number two on the list of the top ten endangered animals who inhabit the Arctic tundra region, right after the Arctic fox at number one. The narwhal,

Patrick remembered, was number seven, the walrus number ten.

Monty opened a tin of condensed milk and stuck his tongue inside.

'Delicious.' He licked his lips and sighed heavily. 'Lord Byron. Now there's a poet I haven't thought of in a while. What a dear boy he was. Most flamboyant of the Romantics. Partial to a little scandal and aristocratic excess. Now *there* was a chap who knew how to live.' Monty closed his eyes and began to quietly recite.

'*What is the end of Fame? 'tis but to fill*
A certain portion of uncertain paper…'

Monty paused. He sniffed and wiped a tear from his eye with his paw.

Patrick picked up his rucksack. He thought it best he left Monty alone. He didn't want to worry him with his thoughts about Mr Crankly and the possibility of the entire polar bear species becoming extinct by 2050.

Sometimes, Patrick thought, it was best to just let someone recite poetry in a chest freezer, even if they were endangered, hungry and one thousand five hundred and ninety-seven miles from home or, as Patrick's dad liked to say, *up the creek without a paddle.*

20

Patrick was sure it wasn't just his imagination: everyone at school on Friday was definitely acting strange around him.

He walked into registration and the group of popular girls who sat over in the left corner by the cupboards had all looked at him and nudged each other. This was very weird. Usually, *those* girls didn't give him a second glance.

When he'd sat down, Gavin came over to him and mumbled very quickly, 'Arnav and me have a lot of respect for you Patrick, but we can't take your side. You understand, don't you? We like our wives.'

Patrick had nodded, confused, but Gavin was already on his way back to his seat. He later wondered if Gavin had said *lives*, not wives, seeing that Patrick was pretty sure Gavin had never had a girlfriend in his life.

Then, Raphael Potts, one of the chess-playing computer coders in Patrick's year, sidled up to Patrick's desk and said in a very low voice, 'Don't forget to put your gum shield in. They should always be worn for contact sports.'

Before Patrick had a chance to ask him what he was talking about, he ran off.

Finally, Sammy came in and sat down next to Patrick. He noticed Sammy was wearing green socks with Snakes and Ladders on them.

'What's going on?' Patrick asked. 'Everyone's acting weird around me.'

Sammy looked at him in disbelief. 'You mean you don't know?'

'No, I don't know anything.'

Sammy shook his head. 'Jake's been telling everyone that you've got it in for him, that you got him in serious trouble with old Plimmy and that now you want a fight.'

'A fight?' Patrick looked at Sammy. 'Why would I want a fight?'

'I don't know. He's told everyone.'

'When?' Patrick asked. 'When does he want a fight?'

'Next Tuesday,' Sammy said. 'After school.'

'Where?'

'Top field.'

Patrick couldn't believe this. He'd have no chance in a fight against Jake Sutherland, the boy who supposedly did a hundred press-ups before school every morning and who pushed boys over on the rugby field like he was swatting away flies. Jake's arm muscles were probably bigger than Patrick's thighs.

'I bet he wants the fight to be Tuesday because he wants time to let word get around,' Patrick said. 'He wants to make sure there'll be a big audience to watch him beat me to a pulp.'

Sammy didn't say anything to this which wasn't particularly comforting but at least he didn't try to offer Patrick any false hope.

'I feel really bad,' Sammy said. 'I was the one who knocked on the staffroom door. I got Jake into trouble.' Sammy swallowed hard. 'We should tell him that. I should go for the fight with him, not you.'

'No,' Patrick said, firmly. 'I'm not letting you do that. If you weren't hanging around with me then he'd never have started picking on you. It's *me* he doesn't like.'

'I know. I just feel bad.'

'Don't,' Patrick said. He was trying to be brave but his voice didn't sound very convincing.

Patrick tried to think how Monty might handle this situation. Most likely, he'd take it in his stride, like he seemed to do with everything else. He'd probably wave his paw in the air and tell Patrick that everything would be *just fine, old chap*.

That was all very well for Monty. He wasn't the one who was about to be pummelled into the ground by a boy who did a hundred press-ups in front of his bedroom mirror every morning whilst listening to *Eye of The Tiger* (this is how Patrick imagined Jake doing them anyway).

Of course Monty could just eat Jake.

Patrick imagined bringing Monty to school on the day of his fight. Monty would hide behind a tree. Patrick would whistle just as Jake was about to hit him. Monty would jump out and eat Jake whole whilst everyone watched, spitting out his Kickers shoes.

Patrick knew that could never happen. Bringing Monty to school would put Monty in danger.

He thought of his parents coming to visit him in hospital after his fight. The stress of his injuries would surely drive his parents even further apart, not to mention the financial fallout from Patrick's plastic surgery bill. He wasn't sure the NHS would fork out for his new post-Jake-Sutherland-beating face. Patrick knew the NHS were stretched. It came up often on the news. Patrick's uncle Barry had had his knee replaced last year and, although he had come out of hospital two days later talking about nothing but how 'blooming fantastic' all the doctors and nurses had been, he had been told to strengthen his new knee at home using an oven glove and

two bags of frozen peas, one in each side. Hardly high-tech.

'Dude.' Sammy clicked his fingers in front of Patrick's eyes. 'Where'd you go?'

'Sorry,' Patrick said. 'Do you know Jake does a hundred press-ups and sit-ups every morning before school?'

Sammy didn't reply. He was staring at his pencil case. 'Man, oh, man,' he said, shaking his head. 'This is bad.'

Patrick didn't disagree.

'Hey,' Sammy said. 'Maybe you could hench up?'

'Hench up?' Patrick said, looking at Sammy in disbelief. 'People spend *months* training for marathons or boxing matches. I've got a few days. Jake's been doing his press-ups since *Year Five*.'

Sammy shrugged. 'My mum only goes to Pilates once a week but she says any exercise is better than no exercise.'

'I guess…'

Sammy punched Patrick on the arm.

'Ouch!'

Sammy rolled his eyes. 'You couldn't even take that? Jeez. You are seriously in for it.'

Patrick looked at Sammy and then they both started laughing.

The bell rang and they began to reluctantly get up and make their way out of the classroom.

'You're right,' Patrick said. 'I should hench up. You can help me. We'll do it together. Why don't you come round tomorrow afternoon?'

'Yeah, that would be cool. The coming over to yours part I mean, not the exercise part.' Sammy shuddered a little. His face brightened as he thought of something. 'I guess I could be your trainer, like Mr Miagi.'

'Who?'

'From *The Karate Kid*,' Sammy said.

'Never seen it.'

'Man, you need some serious movie education.'

Patrick grinned. 'We should have a film night – when I'm recovering from my plastic surgery.'

Sammy smiled. 'Yeah, okay. I'll bring it over, and the first sequel, but not the others. They're really bad. And popcorn. You can't watch a movie without popcorn.'

21

The rest of the school day passed uneventfully. Patrick was aware of hushed conversations and finger-pointing but Jake kept away from him, probably to build tension.

Patrick couldn't stop thinking about the fight.

He walked home from school quickly. It was windy and the wind made his ears hurt. He pulled the hood of his coat up and had to step around a fallen tree branch when he reached the traffic lights.

In the Co-op, he realised he only had

enough money left for two tins of sardines and two tins of condensed milk. Never mind. Tomorrow was Saturday and he'd hopefully be able to wash more cars over the weekend. As much as washing cars wasn't the ideal way to spend a weekend, Patrick had to admit that working to feed Monty, and even just thinking about Monty, was a good distraction from everything else; from Jake, and from all the sadness that seemed to be lingering around the house right now. Even if his morning might be spent washing cars, he was at least going to hang out with Sammy in the afternoon.

When he went into the garage, Monty was back in the chest freezer. He was listening to music and, for some reason, wearing sunglasses. An old pair belonging to Patrick's dad. He was drumming his claws against the side of the freezer in time to the music, bobbing his head up and down, and making a funny growling noise which, after a moment or two, Patrick realised was polar bear humming.

Monty lifted the sunglasses. 'An accidental holiday isn't an accidental holiday without a tune or two,' he said, heaving himself up out of the freezer.

Patrick looked around to see where the music was coming from.

Monty had found Patrick's mum and dad's old CDs. They didn't have any CDs in the house anymore as they streamed all the music they wanted digitally but they hadn't got around to taking their CDs to the charity shop and had left them, along with the box of books, in the garage. Monty had put one of the CDs into the very old Radio/CD player that Patrick's dad used when he was sorting through things in the garage or decorating.

'Dire Straits,' Monty explained. 'An excellent band.'

Patrick thought this was an apt choice

given Monty's current situation but he said nothing. He watched as Monty spun the volume dial with a claw, turning the music up. He recognised the song. His dad had played it a few times. It was called *Twisting by the Pool*.

Monty put his sunglasses back on. He stood up on his hind legs and began to move in time to the music. He grabbed an open tin of condensed milk (one of yesterday's he must have saved) took a swig, then began to shake his huge behind and wiggle his tail. He twisted up and down, once going so low Patrick thought he was going to fall backwards and end up sitting on the garage floor, or in one of the empty storage crates. He held his tin of condensed milk out in front of him like it was a martini.

Patrick shook his head and took the new tins from his rucksack.

Monty looked at them. 'Slim pickings today,' he said loudly over the music. 'Not much of a catch.'

'There'll be more tomorrow,' Patrick promised, hoping this would be true.

Monty lumbered over and patted Patrick on the shoulder. 'That's the spirit. Tomorrow's another day, old bean. There's always a seal somewhere on the horizon. Don't let it all get you down.'

'I'll try,' Patrick replied, unhappily.

'My dear boy, why so glum?'

Patrick sighed. 'There's a boy at school who wants to have a fight with me.'

'Fisticuffs?' Monty said, raising an eyebrow. 'Whatever for? Is it over a seal?'

'No,' Patrick said loudly, as the music was still playing. 'It isn't over a seal. 'It's because, well… I think he just doesn't like me.'

Monty shook his head. 'There is a well-known theory in the animal kingdom that human beings are completely insane. This does not disprove the theory.'

Patrick thought there was probably some truth in this.

Monty turned the CD player off then began to move his paws very quickly in front of his face.

'What are you doing?' Patrick asked, alarmed.

'Wing Chun.'

'Wing what?'

'It's a traditional Chinese martial art. I can teach you, if you like.'

'It's okay,' Patrick said, sighing. 'No offence but I don't think it will do much good.'

Monty put his paws down. 'Probably for

the best. I'm only a novice myself. The pandas have a much better grasp of it.'

'That makes sense. Anyway,' Patrick sighed, 'I was thinking about just getting a bit fitter. You know, so I can dart out the way of Jake's punches.'

'Ah, you mean *exercise*,' Monty grinned, showing his teeth. 'Well, why didn't you say so, old chap? *That,* I can help with.'

Monty went over to the CD player, switched it back on, turned up the volume then stood in front of Patrick with his hands on his hips. Pulling his sunglasses back down over his eyes he said, 'Call me *Mr Motivator.*'

Monty stood on his hind legs then began to do squats in time with the music. 'Come on, dear boy. Keep up.'

Patrick was confused. 'Am I supposed to copy you?

'Move that body!' Monty boomed at him in response.

194

Patrick reluctantly began to copy Monty's squats. He felt like a bit of a wally.

Monty grabbed the two full, un-opened tins of condensed milk and handed them to Patrick. 'Now — bicep curls! One, two three, four. That's it old sport. Come on — I've seen more muscle on a herring's kneecap!'

Patrick grabbed the tins and looked at his biceps. Monty was probably right, although he didn't think herrings had kneecaps. He tried to keep up with Monty who was holding his own tins. Monty's tins were empty, not that Monty needed to strengthen his biceps. Patrick suspected Monty could push a small car, a seal, or a twelve-year-old boy, over with one front leg if he really wanted too. He looked pretty strong.

The CD moved onto the next track.

My favourite,' Monty said. 'Come on, let's do the walk of life!'

Monty was now wiggling his huge behind whilst cross-stepping to the left, and then to the right. 'Shake it to the left, now shake it to the right!'

22

On Saturday morning Patrick went out into Cherry Tree Close with his bucket, sponge and cloth. This time one of the Simons (specky Simon – the one who wore glasses) was at home and he agreed to having his Mazda MX-5 washed. Mrs Abidi agreed too (she had a Peugeot) and, by eleven o'clock, Patrick had ten pounds in his pocket.

He texted Sammy. *Got to pop in the Co-op and get something. Can you meet me there?*

Okay. Sammy replied.

At one o'clock, Patrick set off for the Co-op where he picked up ten tins of sardines.

He was making his way over to the counter with the tins, concentrating very hard on not dropping them all, when he walked straight into someone.

'Oh, sorry.' Patrick looked up. His eyes widened. He had just accidentally walked into Mr Crankly.

Mr Crankly stood back, growling. He brushed his jacket down with his hand as if Patrick had made it dirty, and looked steadily at him.

Up close Mr Crankly's face was even meaner and harder. He had grey stubble around his chin. His eyes were small and narrow and Patrick watched as they moved slowly down to his fish. Mr Crankly looked at all the tinned fish and made that low growling noise at the back of his throat.

'I don't like secrets,' he said.

Patrick blinked. He didn't know what to

say. He opened his mouth but no sound came out.

'Secrets,' Mr Crankly continued, 'are a withholding of information. Important information. Information people should know about.'

'I… I don't know what you mean.'

Mr Crankly stepped forward, his face so close to Patrick's he could smell the strong Fisherman's Friend mint Mr Crankly was sucking on. He knew the mint was a Fishermen's Friend as he could see the open packet poking out of the top pocket of Mr Crankly's jacket.

Mr Crankly crunched the mint loudly. 'Oh, I think you know *exactly* what I mean. I think you're hiding something, Pipsqueak, and I intend to find out what it is.' He waggled a finger at Patrick. 'There's something fishy about you, boy. I'm watching you.' Mr

Crankly grunted then walked off towards the fridges.

Patrick wasn't going to hang around. He went straight to the checkouts. His legs felt wobbly and his thoughts were all jumbled but he knew he had to keep Monty safe from Mr Crankly.

As he was walking out of the doors, with his bag full of fish, Sammy pulled up on his bike. He hopped off and walked over, wheeling the bike. 'Hey, would you rather lick Mrs Stinker's armpit or chew on her old yellow toenail clipping?'

Patrick smiled. He felt his shoulders relax. Despite all his problems, here was Sammy being his normal self.

Mrs Tinker was their History teacher. They called her Mrs Stinker as she had hygiene issues.

Patrick made a face. 'They're both totally gross. I definitely wouldn't want to lick Mrs

200

Stinker's armpit but then I suppose you could choke on the toenail.'

'I hadn't thought of that… I'll go with the armpit. So are you ready for our training session?'

'I guess so.' Patrick wondered, now, why he had agreed to it. He had secretly hoped Sammy might have forgotten and that they could spend the afternoon playing video games and eating toasted cheese sandwiches. He couldn't tell Sammy he'd exercised yesterday with the polar bear who was living in his garage.

As they walked in the direction of Patrick's house, Sammy peered inside Patrick's bag. He looked confused. 'I guess you must *really* like tinned sardines.'

'Yeah,' Patrick said. 'They're erm… good for the brain. You know – oily fish.'

'I suppose.' Sammy rubbed his chin. 'I don't like sardines much. I don't mind salmon though. Salmon's nice. Very pink. You know, pink used to be a boy's colour.'

'Really?'

'Yep. Red was seen as a strong colour for men – soldiers' jackets and all that. Pink was a lighter version than red so worn by boys. Blue was for girls. It was seen as prettier. But then it switched over. It's all a bit silly really. I quite like pink.' Sammy pulled up his trouser leg to reveal a neon pink sock.

Patrick pretended to shield his eyes. He ran backwards, away from Sammy. 'Put them away! My eyes are burning. I need sunglasses!'

'Ha. Funny,' Sammy called to him. 'It's not my fault if you can't appreciate true style.' He caught up with Patrick and they continued to walk together, turning into Cherry Tree Close.

'There's something I should tell you,' Patrick said as they approached his house.

202

'My mum's been feeling a bit sad recently. She's in, but you might not see her. My dad's away and no one's done much tidying.'

Sammy shrugged. 'That's alright. My mum's a real clean freak so everyone else's houses always look messy to me.'

Patrick frowned. He wasn't sure that was what Sammy was supposed to say but never mind.

'You must be pretty sad too though,' Sammy said, 'about your sister, I mean.'

Patrick stopped at the end of his drive. He hadn't really thought about his own sadness, he'd only been worried about his mum, and his parents deciding they couldn't be together anymore.

'I guess. A bit. Maybe.' he said.

'So you're an only child then? Like me. No other brothers or sisters?'

'Nope,' Patrick said, rummaging around in his pocket for the door key. 'It's just me.'

'Yeah, I sometimes wonder if I'm a throwback to the one-child policy or something.'

Patrick had managed to find his key. 'What?'

'So for thirty years in China, parents were only allowed to have one child. There were exceptions, like if you lived in the countryside and had a girl you were allowed to try for a boy, but mostly people only had one kid. You got a special certificate if you stuck to the rules and just had one. My parents were both only children. Maybe it was hard to break the habit. Or maybe my parents just knew they'd peaked when they saw how awesome I was.'

Patrick grinned. 'Come on,' he said. 'Let's go inside.'

23

Patrick was surprised to find his mum in the kitchen. She was dressed in leggings and a sweatshirt. She'd clipped her hair up and she was wearing earrings, the earrings Patrick's dad had bought her a couple of Christmases ago. This, Patrick thought, had to be a good sign. His mum hadn't worn earrings for ages and you wouldn't wear the earrings your husband gave you if you were going to break up, would you?

'Hello.' Patrick's mum was clearly surprised to see Sammy standing in the kitchen. She gave him a *really* big smile.

Patrick hadn't brought a friend home for ages, not since Tommy was last around.

'This is Sammy,' Patrick said, hoping Sammy wouldn't mention any of the things he'd just told him about his mum being sad, but Sammy only said, 'Hi, Mrs Jolly.'

Patrick's mum laughed. 'Call me Jessica.'

'Jessica Jolly,' Sammy said. 'Nice alliteration.'

'Thanks,' his mum said, still smiling. 'Are you in Patrick's classes? I'm always telling him he can bring friends back. He used to have friends over all the time. I guess things are different at secondary school. Maybe it's not cool to have friends over anymore.'

'Mum…' Patrick said, rubbing his head.

'Oh, I wouldn't say that,' Sammy said. 'Hanging out at other people's houses is one of my all-time favourite occupations.'

Patrick's mum smiled. 'Well, why don't you guys help yourself to some lentil crisps? Patrick's always starving after school.'

'I'm famished,' Sammy replied, making Patrick's mum laugh again.

Patrick was surprised. His mum was acting, well, like his mum. Her thoughts weren't all inside her today. She was out of bed, not on the sofa, and she'd showered. Her hair was still a little bit wet.

'I guess I'll leave you to it then.' Patrick's mum moved towards the back door and opened it. 'You help yourself to whatever you want. I just need to go out to the garage and—'

'Whoa,' Patrick said, rushing towards the door and pushing it closed. 'What do you need to go to the garage for?'

His mum looked surprised. 'I thought I might paint the spare room before your dad gets home on Wednesday, then maybe move his desk in there. I thought he'd like to have his office back.'

Patrick blinked. His mum hadn't called the

spare room 'the spare room' for ages. She'd called it 'Evie-Ann's room'. They all had. Patrick's dad had moved his desk into the garage a few months ago. *It's only temporary*, he'd said. *I'm going to build a shed at the end of the garden sometime soon, turn it into an office.*

Patrick couldn't believe his mum wanted to paint Evie-Ann's room. She often went and sat in there. It was still full of the brand-new things they'd bought for Evie-Ann.

His mum put a hand on his shoulder as if she knew he was thinking all this.

'Which paint do you need?' Patrick asked.

'There's a tin of that mushroomy colour. You know, the one we used for the downstairs loo.'

'I'll get it later,' Patrick said. 'You hate the garage. It's cold. And last time I was in there I saw a *really big* spider.'

Sammy looked from Patrick to Patrick's mum.

His mum looked alarmed. 'Really?'

Patrick nodded. 'It was probably a tarantula.'

'Oh, yes,' Sammy said, chipping in. 'I hear there are lots of tarantulas around at this time of year. I saw it on *Newsround*. They sneak into the country by clinging to bananas or hiding under melons. They like to live in cold, dark places where nobody ever goes, like garages.'

Patrick's mum shivered. 'Okay, then. If you could grab it for me later, Patrick, that would be really helpful.'

Once the backdoor was safely closed, Patrick went to the cupboard and grabbed a couple of bags of lentil crisps and two cereal bars.

'You can take them upstairs, boys, but no crumbs. Crumbs might attract mice, or spiders!'

'I don't think spiders eat lentil crisps, Mum.'

'Well, you never know.'

Upstairs, Sammy sat down on Patrick's orange desk chair. He spun all the way around. 'Cool poster,' he said, pointing at the stoat photograph on the wall next to Patrick's football calendar.

'Yeah. Actually, it's a photograph. My dad took it.'

'Really?'

'He's a wildlife photographer.'

Sammy looked impressed. 'That's such a cool job. My dad just does something boring with other people's money. We get lots of holidays though,' he said thoughtfully, 'like four a year.'

'Wow. We don't go on holiday so much. Unless you count camping.'

Sammy grinned. 'I like camping. It's more fun than some of the hotels we go to. My mum wants to spend all day in the spa and my dad wants to spend all day on his laptop.

210

Ha. I end up sitting by the pool on my own drinking too much Fanta.' Sammy grinned. 'Or else my parents enrol me in some kids' day camp where you have to wear a T-shirt with a big smiley face on the front that says "Sun World Kids' Club", or something like that.'

Patrick knew Sammy was just trying to make him feel better. 'Sounds terrible,' he said, smiling.

'What was all that about downstairs. The garage? I tried to help you out. What are you hiding in there?'

'Oh, nothing,' Patrick said, quickly. 'I mean, thanks for your help, but it's nothing. Just a garage.'

Sammy looked unconvinced. 'Have you got a tramp in there? Are you building a spaceship?'

'Really it's nothing.'

Sammy shrugged then stood up and

looked around the room. 'I guess we should start training then.'

Patrick wondered how they were going to do this. He didn't own any weights. He couldn't face the thought of doing press-ups. He'd feel like a failure if he only managed ten when Jake could apparently do a hundred.

As if he had read Patrick's mind, Sammy pointed at Patrick. 'Fifty press-ups, Jolly!'

Patrick shook his head. 'I don't think so.'

Sammy folded his arms across his chest and put on a strict, deep voice. 'Another fifty for disobedience. Now drop and show me what you've got, you filthy maggot. I run my unit how I run my unit.'

Patrick rolled his eyes but he was smiling. 'I'm not doing fifty press-ups. We'll go for a run. *Together.*'

'A run?'

'It's cardio. Just as important.'

Sammy made a face. 'Fine.' He turned and looked in the mirror on Patrick's wardrobe doors. 'You talkin' to me?' he said, pointing at himself.

Patrick had to admit, Sammy was a little strange at times.

Sammy was wearing jeans and a jumper so Patrick lent him a pair of tracksuit trousers and the sweatshirt his Aunt Pru in Dorset had given him for Christmas. It had a picture of the Cookie Monster on the front and said, *Why You Delete Cookies?* Patrick was in sports trousers and his favourite blue hoody so he didn't bother changing.

'We're just going for a run, Mum!' Patrick called out when they were down by the front door.

'A run?' his mum said, in a puzzled kind of way, but it was too late, they were opening the door.

'We'll go out of Cherry Tree Close, along

Windmill Street, down to the church, to the canal, then back.'

'Dude. That's far.'

'It's like, fifteen minutes.'

They started to jog along the road.

Mrs Wilkinson was in her drive, lifting the smallest member of the Wilkinson family, baby Florence, out of her car seat. She stopped to wave at Patrick, and Florence waved too, dropping her plastic spoon onto the driveway then looking confused.

Patrick waved back at them.

'Man,' Sammy said, already breathing heavily, 'why would anyone run when you can just *walk*. I mean, it can't be good for you, can it?'

'Don't talk,' Patrick said, as they jogged out of Cherry Tree Close. 'It'll be easier on your lungs.'

'Sitting down would be easier on my lungs,' Sammy replied, gasping for breath.

They ran out of Cherry Tree Close and along Windmill Road. It became easier as they got into a rhythm.

'Nearly there,' Patrick said, when they saw the church and then, finally, the canal.

As they crossed the road, Sammy started to hum *Chariots of Fire* although he was clearly finding it difficult to hum and run at the same time. He stopped running then began again, this time running in slow motion.

Patrick looked back at Sammy. He couldn't help laughing. Sammy looked pretty strange doing his slow motion run and pretending to cross an imaginary finish line.

When they reached the bench by the canal, Sammy sat down. He wiped his forehead whilst Patrick stretched his hamstrings.

'Doesn't it feel *kind of* good for us?' Patrick asked.

'No,' Sammy said, still catching his breath.

'We should turn back now. Keep momentum up.'

Sammy stood up, thinking of something. 'Hey, how about we Uber back? I've got the app, for emergencies. My mum set it up.'

'We're not Ubering back', Patrick said firmly. 'This isn't an emergency. It's a run.'

Sammy sighed and stood up. They began to jog slowly. 'I really wish you had more time to train before the fight,' he said between breaths.

'I know,' Patrick replied. 'Me too. It's probably pointless but I have to try. Otherwise I might as well just lay down on the ground.'

'You could play dead,' Sammy suggested, squeezing his words out in between breaths. 'Like a hedgehog. I saw one in the road once that I thought had been run over. I stopped to look at it but as soon as I moved away it ran off. Hedgehogs move pretty fast.'

216

'I don't think pretending to be a dead hedgehog is the answer,' Patrick said, panting heavily as they reached the turning for Cherry Tree Close. 'But thanks for the suggestion.'

'You're welcome,' Sammy said on an out-breath.

In Cherry Tree Close, a Sainsbury's delivery van was pulling up outside the Wilkinsons'.

As soon as they reached Patrick's house, Sammy stopped and leaned on the fence, catching his breath. Only it wasn't Patrick's fence.

They heard the sound of a window opening behind them.

'Hey, you. Squirt! Get off my fence!'

Patrick and Sammy turned to see Mr Crankly standing at his bay window waving a duster. He'd opened the window in order to shout at them.

'Can't you see the sign!' Mr Crankly yelled.

Sammy and Patrick looked at where Mr

Crankly was pointing. There was a sign saying *Wet Paint*.

'Whoops,' Sammy said, looking at his hands which had a few sticky blobs of white paint on them.

'I'll have to re-paint!' Mr Crankly looked furious; his ears were red again.

Sammy and Patrick quickly darted into Patrick's drive. They watched as Mr Crankly shook his head then pulled his net curtains across and shut the window.

'Jeez,' Sammy whispered. '*Squirt?* That man really knows how to pump a guy's self-esteem.'

'Yeah, he calls me Pipsqueak.'

They looked at each other and began to laugh.

Patrick's mum opened the front door. 'Are you both okay out there?'

'Yeah, Mum,' Patrick said, trying not to choke on his words. 'We're good.'

218

'We're fine, Mrs Jolly.' Sammy was holding onto his stomach, doubled up, this time not from exertion but because he was laughing so hard. He looked at his hands again which only made him laugh more.

'We're coming in now, Mum,' Patrick said, trying to catch his breath. 'You can leave the door open.'

Patrick's mum shook her head a little but she was smiling. She left them too it, which was a good thing as Sammy had started hiccupping. 'I've got a (hic) stitch (hic),' he said.

This set them both off laughing again.

Patrick thought of Mr Crankly shouting at Sammy and how things seemed so much less scary when you had a friend around.

He felt sure he could trust Sammy after all.

'Hey,' Patrick said. 'I've got something to show you. 'It's in the garage. Come on.' He shut the front door. 'Let's go around the back.'

'I knew there was something in there! It's a spaceship, right?'

'Ha. No. Oh, wait, do you want to wash your hands first?'

'Nah. It's only a few spots. It's pretty much dry. I'd rather see your spaceship.'

24

As they approached the garage Patrick felt worried about Sammy and Monty meeting. He didn't want to put either of them in danger. He didn't want Monty to think he'd brought him lunch in the form of a schoolboy. Neither did he want Sammy to be so freaked out that he immediately rushed to tell his parents, or worse – the police.

Patrick opened the garage door. He pushed Sammy ahead of him and shut the door quickly behind them. He didn't want Sammy to run up the garden screaming.

Patrick stepped in front of Sammy, ready to make the introductions.

Monty wasn't there.

Patrick stared at the empty chest freezer as Sammy stood, a confused expression on his face.

Where was Monty? How could he have disappeared?

Patrick looked from left to right. He went over to the freezer. He stood in the middle of the garage scratching his head.

'Didn't you want to show me something?'

'Um…'

Patrick thought maybe Sammy just couldn't see Monty for some reason but then of course that would mean that if Monty was in the garage, Patrick would still be able to see him. Only he couldn't. So that meant Monty was missing. He felt his chest tighten.

Sammy still looked confused. This, Patrick

thought, was what you would call a Totally Awkward Moment.

'This is our garage,' Patrick said, sounding like an idiot. 'I thought that, um, seeing that you've seen the rest of the house, you should see the garage. That's all I wanted to show you.'

'Oh, I see…' Sammy looked disappointed. 'Well… Sure. It's a great garage, Patrick,' he said, making an effort to look around. 'Really, um, garagy.'

'My mum always says we should give anyone who visits the house for the first time "the grand tour". I guess I didn't want you to miss out.'

'Ha,' Sammy said, thinking Patrick had made a joke, although it was true – Patrick's mum did say that.

'Actually, talking of mums, mine doesn't like me cycling in the dark, even though I've got lights. I should probably get going.'

'Right,' Patrick said, relieved. He had to find Monty. 'Good idea. You should probably get going. Yes, *now* would be good. Before it gets dark.' Patrick was trying to act normal but all he could think about was Monty and where he might be. He imagined Monty out on the streets being captured and thrown into a cage.

Sammy gave Patrick a confused look. 'Okay then. See you at school, I guess.'

Patrick and Sammy went out onto the drive where Sammy picked up his bike.

'Are you sure you're alright, Patrick?' Sammy asked.

'Fine,' he said, trying to smile.

'Well, okay then...'

Once Sammy had gone, Patrick checked the garage again, just to make sure Monty wasn't there. He wasn't. Then he checked the garden, including behind the bonfire which was really the only place Monty

could be without being seen. He wasn't there either.

Patrick went out into Cherry Tree Close and looked up and down the street. One of the Simons (the one without the glasses) was pulling out of his drive in the Mazda. Rudolph was in the passenger seat, looking excited. They didn't see him.

Mrs Wilkinson was standing on her doorstep chatting to the Sainsbury's delivery man who was holding a mug of tea she must have made for him. They appeared to be deep in conversation. Perhaps they knew each other. The delivery man had left the back doors of the van open and the van was rocking slightly. Patrick crept closer. He peered through the open doors.

Monty was inside the van on his hind legs, pulling something down from the top of a crate – a cardboard box. He opened the box and pulled out a Black Forest gateau.

He smiled then pushed his nose straight in, munching happily.

Patrick crept along the pavement towards the van. Monty saw him and waved. He had a blob of cream on his nose.

'What a tip off this was,' Monty said in a low, excited voice. 'Little Kevin was right on the money on this one. I've never had much use for tree-climbing creatures but that squirrel certainly knew where a bear could find lunch. Mind you, I did have him by the tail…'

'Monty! We've got to get you back to the garage!'

Patrick flattened his back against the inside of the van door. He peeped around. Mrs Wilkinson and the driver were still chatting. Luckily they were facing away from the van but the driver was draining the last of his tea. Weren't those drivers always on a tight schedule? What if he shut the doors when

226

Monty was still inside and drove him back to the depot? How would he find Monty then? That would be the end of Monty. He could see the headline now. *Sainsbury's delivery driver finds polar bear in van. Bear shot for fear of human safety.*

He could still hear Mrs Wilkinson and the delivery driver talking.

'Well, we were lucky,' Mrs Wilkinson was saying. 'We bought at the right time. Prices have really gone up around here.'

'Oh, yes they've shot up,' he heard the delivery driver say.

Good. They were talking about boring grown-up things which meant he probably had a little time.

Monty was still eating the cake. He had chocolate all around his mouth like a toddler. 'Must we go?' he said, between mouthfuls, so that it sounded more like: *Mush ee ow?*

'Yes! Right now, Monty!'

Monty sighed and lumbered over to the end of the van, tucking a packet of frozen haddock under his arm.

Patrick peeped around the doors. They were still talking but the delivery man was handing his clipboard to Mrs Wilkinson to sign.

There was no chance of hiding Monty. They'd have to make a run for it. Patrick's house was only three houses away.

'On the count of three,' Patrick said, 'we run back to my garden. As *quietly* as you can. Stay low – behind the parked cars.'

'Don't worry, old bean. These padded paws are meant for creeping up on unsuspecting prey. I'll put my claws away and you won't hear a thing. Silent as a mouse, that's me. Although, in my opinion, mice are rather noisy, given their size.'

'No more talking! Are you ready, Monty?'

'Always, old sport. Always.'

'One, two, three!'

Monty climbed out of the van and ambled along the road. Patrick tried to usher Monty along, not daring to look behind him at Mrs Wilkinson and the delivery driver. He expected to hear a cry of alarm, maybe a scream. There he was pushing a large chocolate-covered polar bear along the pavement in broad daylight.

'See you next week then,' the driver called out.

'Cheerio Dan,' Mrs Wilkinson replied. 'Give my love to Sophie.'

Patrick and Monty turned into the driveway. Patrick opened the garage and Monty lumbered inside just as he heard the van doors close.

Phew.

The engine started. Dan the driver obviously hadn't looked inside and seen what was left of the Black Forest gateau on the floor.

Patrick quickly shut the garage door behind Monty. The van was turning towards him. Dan the driver saw Patrick, smiled, and gave him a wave. Patrick lifted his hand to wave back. He tried to smile but his face felt frozen. He could feel his heart beating. He leaned against the garage and took a few deep, slow breaths: *in through the nose, out through the nose...* (they *had* actually had a yoga lesson in P.E. once).

He had better go back in the garage. He had almost forgotten to get the paint. He couldn't believe what a close call that was. What did Monty think he was playing at? As if Patrick didn't have enough to deal with.

Monty was sitting casually by the freezer licking his paws as if nothing had happened. Patrick ignored Monty whilst he found the paint for his mum. This must be the one. It

was definitely the one they'd used for the downstairs loo.

'Doing a spot of decorating?' Monty asked.

'Yes,' Patrick said, grumpily. 'Look, Monty, why can't you just stay in the garage?'

'Fresh air, old sport. Freedom, books, flowers and the——'

'Well, you won't be getting any fresh air if you get captured, will you.'

'Oh, I wouldn't worry——'

Patrick gripped the handle of the paint tin. '*Someone* has to worry. Anyone would think you enjoyed putting yourself in danger and causing trouble for me. If something bad happens to you, it will be all my fault. You really are quite selfish, you know. I wish you hadn't come here. I wish you'd swum back to Greenland.'

Monty looked hurt. He lifted the lid of the freezer and attempted to squash himself inside. 'Well, as you wish.'

'That's just it. Nothing's *as I wish*. No one cares about what I wish for. In fact, what I really wish is that you'd go home and leave me alone.'

Patrick found he was shaking a little. He didn't wait to hear Monty's response. He took his tin of paint, turned and left the garage, slamming the door behind him.

25

On Monday morning, second lesson, they'd had rugby on the bottom field with Mr Larson. It was a grey and drizzly morning. Everyone got wet whilst Mr Larson stood on the field in his waterproof jacket and trousers, shouting at them from beneath his umbrella.

Once the lesson was over and Patrick was in the changing rooms with the others, he shoved his muddy P.E. clothes into his kit bag and began to put his uniform on. His thoughts were on Monty as usual. He couldn't afford another near miss like Saturday. He hadn't bothered going to check on Monty yesterday. He'd felt too mad at him. Instead, he'd sat on the sofa most of the day watching Netflix whilst his mum slept.

Patrick realised that almost everyone else had left the changing rooms, everyone except Jake, Luke and Caleb who were messing around in the corner, and a few others who were picking up the last of their things. Patrick grabbed his bag and headed for the doors but when he tried to leave, Caleb blocked his way by putting an arm across the door.

'Jake wants a word with you.'

Caleb let the last few boys out: Arnav, Gavin and Tomasz. They kept their heads down. Patrick looked around but couldn't see Sammy anywhere. He must have gone out already. He turned and saw Luke and Jake still over by the benches. They were now the only four boys left in the changing rooms. He could hear Mr Larson outside in the corridor

234

talking to their drama teacher, Miss Patwari. There had been rumours that Mr Larson had asked her out a few times but that she always said no.

Before he could think about what was happening they were on him. Caleb had grabbed his arms and Jake and Luke were pushing him into a corner.

'Oi, get off,' Patrick heard himself say, his voice muffled as he spoke into the shoulder of Caleb's blazer.

He wondered if they were going to beat him up. But Jake wanted a fight tomorrow after school, didn't he? And who would see them in here? Patrick thought the whole point was that Jake wanted everyone to see how strong and mean he was. This didn't make any sense.

'Get his legs,' Jake was saying.

Patrick felt himself being lifted off the ground. 'Hey!' He was being pushed against the wall. 'What are you doing? I thought you wanted a fight tomorrow?' Patrick's voice sounded small, smaller than he would have liked, more afraid than he would have liked. He felt like he had a rock in the pit of his stomach.

Jake just laughed. 'Think of this as a prequel, Brolly. Peg him.'

Before he knew what was happening Luke and Caleb were lifting him. He felt his blazer being yanked. They'd hooked it over the peg above his head. Luke and Caleb were still holding him. Patrick tried to wriggle free but it was useless, they just increased their grip on his legs. He was beginning to feel dizzy. Time seemed to have sped up; it was all happening too quickly.

Jake stood in front of him. He was so close Patrick could feel Jake's breath on his neck. It smelled of cheesy crisps.

'Listen, Brolly. You'd better not try any

236

funny stuff – telling teachers or anything like that.'

Patrick shook his head. He gulped down a few deep breaths. 'No.' His voice sounded squeaky.

Jake smiled, showing his teeth, and reminding Patrick of Bruce, the shark in *Finding Nemo*.

'Good,' Jake said. 'I'm glad you understand. Cos it'll be a whole lot worse for you if you do. If Plimmy turns up tomorrow, I'll know it's you who's said something.'

'I understand,' Patrick squeaked. His blazer was beginning to dig into his underarms, making his fingers tingle.

'See you tomorrow, Brolly,' Jake said. 'Top field. Three forty-five.' Luke and Caleb let go of his legs. They were walking out of the changing room.

As soon as Jake, Luke and Caleb had gone, Mr Larson came straight in.

'Jolly! Stop messing around on that peg. Get out of here!'

'But, sir—'

'I don't want to hear it, Jolly.'

Patrick eventually managed to unhook himself. He gathered up his things whilst Mr Larson stood glaring at him. Perhaps Miss Patwari had said no again.

Patrick didn't want to bump into Jake and Luke and Caleb at the lockers so he sat on a bench by the arts block and waited for the bell. Luckily the bench wasn't too wet, despite the drizzle. Not that he cared that much.

Patrick felt weary, and all sort of knotted inside. He knew this weary feeling meant it was probably time for him to tell someone about Jake and his mean sidekicks. That's what it said on the posters he'd seen around school: *If you're being bullied, tell an adult.* Patrick now realised this applied to him. They'd been picking on him for ages and it was only

getting harder to ignore. He also knew he couldn't tell on Jake or things might become *a whole lot worse,* as Jake had just warned him. Telling an adult was likely to get him beaten to a pulp.

He couldn't tell his mum because she'd worry. He couldn't tell his dad because bringing another problem into the house might make his dad want to run further than Scotland. Where was further than the Scottish Highlands anyway? If he went any further he'd be in the Outer Hebrides, or Iceland, or *Greenland.*

Patrick sighed. Why hadn't Monty stopped at the Outer Hebrides where there weren't many people around and where he could have lived in someone's barn until a fishing boat passed. Why did Monty have to come all the way into London where it wasn't safe at all? At least he had thought to swim up the canal. Goodness knows what would have happened if Monty had wandered along the Southbank. He'd probably have stopped to look at the second-hand books, tried to get into the National Theatre to watch a play, or else broken into the aquarium for lunch. Patrick imagined Monty chasing pigeons in Trafalgar Square or being mistaken for a street performer. Maybe he could actually make a decent living as a street performer. Anyway, he was glad it hadn't come to that.

'There you are.' Sammy appeared from around the corner. He was wearing odd socks: one orange, one blue. He sat down next to Patrick. 'I wondered where you'd got to.'

Patrick told Sammy what had happened.

'What a bunch of ignoramuses,' Sammy said.

'And where were you, anyway?' Patrick gripped his P.E. bag.

'What do you mean?'

'In the changing rooms.'

'I don't know. I guess I thought you were behind me.'

'Well, I wasn't.'

Patrick could feel his muscles tensing. It wasn't fair that he'd been put on a peg then shouted at by Mr Larson. It wasn't fair that *he* was the one they always picked on. Suddenly, he didn't want to speak to Sammy anymore. He stood up and turned to Sammy. 'Friends are supposed to look out for each other.'

'Look, Patrick, I didn't realise—'

'I don't care.' Patrick stood up and kicked the bench. He shoved his fists angrily into the pockets of his wonky blazer then began to walk away.

'Hey!' Sammy called after Patrick, causing a couple of girls to look over in their direction.

Patrick ignored Sammy. He made his way towards the arts block doors.

26

When Patrick arrived home from school, the house smelled strongly of paint. He put his rucksack down, took his shoes off and went straight upstairs.

His mum had painted half a wall in Evie-Ann's room, covering the lemon yellow with the light grey mushroomy colour. He noticed she had left the brushes lying on the old sheet she'd placed on the floor, and that the paint lid was off. Patrick put the lid back on the tin. The paint would dry out otherwise.

He went onto the landing then poked his head around his parents' bedroom door. He

could see his mum asleep under the covers. There was a plate of un-touched crackers on her bedside table.

He left her alone and went into his own bedroom.

He sighed and took his blazer and tie off. It had been a horrible day. He hadn't spoken to Sammy since break. Tomorrow was the day of the fight. Now that he'd fallen out with Sammy, there would be no one on his side. No one else in Year Seven would dare stick up for Patrick against Jake. Sammy would have at least been there to check Patrick was still breathing after Jake had finished, and maybe call the ambulance.

And Jake wasn't the only problem.

Patrick decided he would speak to Monty that night. He wasn't going to let Monty distract him with his Oscar Wilde quotes and comments about accidental holidays. He was going to tell Monty, firmly, that it was time for him to be going, and that they *had* to figure out a plan.

It hadn't been *too* difficult to keep his mum out of the garage, but Patrick's dad was coming home on Tuesday and he might go straight in there to put some of his stuff away.

It was lucky that Monty hadn't been seen that night when he went through the wheelie bins, or by Mr Crankly when he ate the koi carp from his pond. Mr Crankly was the kind of person who probably had cameras watching his property, along with intruder alarms.

Monty had got away with living in the garage for over a week. He'd been lucky, but luck inevitably ran out.

Patrick sat on his bed.

He had lost Sammy, his only friend.

Jake was going kill him.

His mum was back under her duvet.

His dad would come home on Tuesday and wish he could go away again.

He didn't know what to do about Monty who probably hated him now anyway.

And, he had no pocket money.

He clenched his fists. He stood up, grabbed Mr Nutkins from the windowsill and hurled him across the room.

Patrick watched as Mr Nutkins hit the wall above the wardrobe then fell down the back of it. He sat staring at the spot on the wall that Mr Nutkins had hit before he'd fallen. Mr Nutkins, the rabbit his parents had given him when he'd been born. Mr Nutkins who had been with him on every holiday and camping trip, who'd been in all his games and most of the family photographs. Mr Nutkins who'd always been there for him, no matter what.

He punched his pillow so hard it hurt his

hand. He wanted to scream but of course he couldn't because his mum would hear.

Instead, he walked over to his wardrobe then got down on his hands and knees and reached into the gap behind. He felt the tip of one of Mr Nutkins' ears. He tugged at the ear. There was the horrible sound of fabric tearing.

Patrick managed to pull Mr Nutkins out but his head was clinging on by a thread. There was a smudge of dust on his belly, a cobweb on his ear and some of his stuffing was popping out of the hole where his head should have been. He no longer looked like the Mr Nutkins he knew and loved.

Patrick stared at Mr Nutkins. He was broken, along with everything else, and it was all his fault.

He got up from the floor and threw Mr Nutkins into his wastepaper basket. Whatever.

He was too old for him anyway. He had real, grown-up things to deal with now.

Patrick took a deep breath then left his room. He peeped around his parents' bedroom door again. 'Mum, are you okay?' He still felt angry although he tried to make his voice sound normal. Of course she wasn't okay. But why couldn't she be okay? Other people's mums were. It just wasn't fair.

Patrick's mum was still under the duvet, her head buried into the pillow.

'I'm sorry,' she whispered.

Patrick went into the room then sat down on the edge of the bed.

'I just wanted to do something,' his mum said into the pillow.

Patrick looked at his mum. She looked sad and worn out. He felt guilty for being angry. His mum needed him and his dad had told him to take care of her.

'It's okay,' he said because he wasn't sure what else to say. He guessed his mum was talking about trying to paint Evie-Ann's room.

'I've sent her things away. We spent so much time choosing them!'

'I know.' Patrick swallowed hard. He wanted to say the right thing. 'I guess they'll make someone else happy, someone else's little sister.'

His mum opened her eyes. She smiled a tiny smile. 'Yes. That's a nice way of thinking about it, Patrick. Thank you.' She turned over and attempted to sit up, pushing the pillow against the headboard. 'I really wanted to paint the room. I wanted to do something nice for your dad. I started, but then I had to come in here to get a tissue. I sat on the bed and then I couldn't paint anymore. I needed to lie down.'

'It doesn't matter,' Patrick said, trying to

248

sound reassuring. 'It's a really good start, Mum.'

Patrick's mum nodded. 'I think I'm just having a bad day.'

So am I! Patrick wanted to say but couldn't.

He thought that every day since Evie-Ann died had been a bad day for his mum but he didn't say this either. Instead he said, 'We'll finish it next weekend, Mum. I'll help you.'

She looked at Patrick and, for the first time in a long time, Patrick thought she was really *looking* at him, not just looking through him as she had been for a while. 'You're pretty handy to have around,' she said, reaching over and patting his arm. 'I reckon we'll hang on to you.'

Patrick smiled. This was the kind of thing his parents were always saying to him, or they used to anyway. They'd look at Patrick, and then each other, and say something silly like. *Hey, he's kind of smart. We should probably* keep him around. Or, *that stork sure did bring us a good'un. We won't be taking him back for a refund anytime soon. Anyway, we've lost the receipt.*

Patrick usually just shook his head when his parents joked like this but today he squeezed his mum's hand and said, 'Reckon I'll hang on to you too, even if you can only paint half a wall.'

His mum laughed, an actual *real* laugh. 'Thanks Patrick.'

She looked down at the duvet and Patrick saw that she was thinking about something sad again. 'I'm not sure I'll be able to cook tonight,' she said. 'I think I need to stay here for a while. 'Will you be able to get yourself something to eat? You won't just have ice cream?'

'No,' Patrick said, thinking that there wasn't any ice cream now anyway since Monty had eaten it all. 'I'll be fine,' he said, feeling calmer. 'I'll make beans on toast.'

'Oh, that's good,' his mum said.

Technically, beans on toast wasn't *actual* cooking, more like heating up, but still, Patrick had always thought that anything that required turning on the oven, or a hob ring, or using the toaster, was cooking.

But first, before he did anything, he had to deal with Monty. It was time for serious words with him.

27

Patrick opened the door.

The garage was empty. Well, not empty exactly. There were a few sardine tins lying around, along with a pyramid of condensed milk tins Monty had put together.

Patrick swallowed hard. 'Monty?' he called, just in case a huge white polar bear was somehow hiding behind a bicycle or a box of tools.

There was no answer.

Patrick felt a sickness in his stomach. Where was Monty this time? And how long had he been gone? He could have left this morning,

252

or even *yesterday*, for all Patrick knew. He could have been gone for hours.

Maybe he hadn't heard anything about a polar bear being shot in a suburban back garden because the authorities wanted to keep it all quiet in order not to alarm civilians. Maybe a government hit squad had made Monty 'disappear'. They'd keep it out of the papers too. It would be awful otherwise. People might think there were more bears on the loose. They wouldn't want to leave their houses, walk their dogs, or even get into their cars. Patrick knew that polar bears had been known to stand up on their hind legs and rock cars. Maybe they thought they were giant sardine tins. That was all you needed on the school run, a sharp-toothed polar bear growling at you through the window.

Then he remembered what he'd said to Monty last night. Maybe Monty had gone for good because Patrick had told him it was what he really wished for. He felt awful. Of course he wanted Monty to get home safely but he'd hoped they could have figured it out together. He hadn't even been able to say goodbye.

Patrick stepped out into the garden. It was beginning to grow dark but that didn't matter. He had to look for Monty just in case, by some miracle, he was still around. He had to *try*.

The fence at the end of the garden was broken.

One of the wooden panels had come away from the post as if something very large had pushed it and gone from Patrick's garden into *Mr Crankly's garden*.

Patrick swallowed hard. He walked to the apple trees and stood looking at the broken fence. Of course a storm could have caused damage like this but there hadn't been a storm for ages, or even harsh enough winds.

Not only that, Patrick's dad only put the fence up last autumn. *That fence will last us ten years*, he'd said.

Patrick took a deep breath then slipped through the gap and into Mr Crankly's garden. He expected an alarm to go off or a spotlight to appear on him but nothing happened.

Mr Crankly's garden was quiet and neat. The lawn was perfectly mowed like a golf course, or a bowling green. The only sound was the steady trickle from the concrete boy weeing into the now fishless pond.

There was a row of plant pots on the patio and not a single weed visible between the paving slabs, unlike Patrick's patio which always sprouted tufts of grass.

Patrick looked around. There was no sign of Monty, only... He noticed something shiny on the grass next to the pond. He crept across the garden towards it.

It was an empty sardine tin.

Then he noticed Mr Crankly's greenhouse. One of the panes of glass was broken. He could see, though, that there was no polar bear inside.

Patrick looked towards the house. The back door to Mr Crankly's conservatory was open slightly. The blinds in the conservatory were down. Patrick couldn't see any sign of Monty but he knew he had to go and investigate.

He crept across the lawn towards the open conservatory door. He wished he'd checked, before going through the fence, whether Mr Crankly's car was in his drive. That would have given him a good indication as to whether Mr Crankly was in the house or not. That's probably what a real secret agent would have done.

He crossed the patio. When he reached the door he slowly pulled it further open and peered inside.

Mr Crankly's conservatory was very cream. Cream walls, cream blinds, two cream sofas and a rattan coffee table with a cream bowl on it filled with nuts. There was a plant in the corner with some kind of small orange fruit hanging from one of the branches. But no sign of Monty.

Except, that is, for the large muddy paw print on Mr Crankly's shiny cream tiles. He hadn't noticed it at first. This meant the Monty was *inside the house.*

Patrick froze. Next to the muddy paw print were several drops of bright red blood. He put his hand over his mouth to stop himself from crying out. What had Mr Crankly done to Monty? Or what had Monty done to Mr Crankly?

It was very quiet in Mr Crankly's conservatory.

Too quiet.

Patrick followed the trail of blood across

the cream tiles towards the door which he imagined must lead to the living room. He knew he was a criminal breaking into his elderly neighbour's house. What would he say if he was caught? *I didn't mean to break in, I was only looking for a polar bear.*

Patrick was worried about Monty but he was worried about himself too. He knew it was legal to defend your property against an intruder in the *heat of the moment.* He'd seen it on one of those true crime programmes. A man had hit a burglar over the head with a vase of flowers, knocking him unconscious, and it was all okay because the man was defending his property and felt himself to be in danger. Would Mr Crankly feel himself in danger if he found Patrick snooping around his house?

Probably.

He'd have his gun or bazooka at the ready. Patrick slowly opened the door to the

living room. He could feel his heart beating in his chest. His hands were clammy.

Mr Crankly's living room was just as Patrick had seen it that day from the doorstep when he'd given Mr Crankly his parcel. The sofas had brown flowery cushions on them and little matching covers over the arms. On the mantelpiece, there was an old photograph of a couple in their wedding outfits. The TV was also very old, like a big box. It was made of wood and had buttons on the front.

The drops of blood were in the living room too. They went all the way across the room to the door. Whose were they? He was very worried about those drops of blood. Then he caught a whiff of that familiar beary smell. It was the smell that had been lingering in the garage all week.

He walked quickly across Mr Crankly's living room hoping his trainers weren't too muddy. He felt an overwhelming sense of dread; his fingers and toes were numb and he hardly dared breathe.

In the hallway, he heard Mr Crankly's voice, low and gravelly.

'Wrong move my furry friend. You've been a worthy opponent. You've fought bravely but there can only be one outcome. You were done for as soon as this began. It's all over for you now. It ends here. This is a trick I learned in the army. I'll make it quick.'

Patrick gasped.

'No!' Monty said.

'No!' Patrick shouted, running into the kitchen towards the voices.

He stopped running when he saw Monty and Mr Crankly at the kitchen table playing chess.

Monty was sitting on a small wooden stool that looked like it might, at any moment, collapse beneath him. He was drinking a tin of condensed milk.

Mr Crankly had a bottle of beer on the table.

Monty looked up. 'My dear boy, he's taken my queen!'

Mr Crankly gave Patrick one of his usual hard stares. He didn't look surprised to see him though.

Patrick felt very strange standing, uninvited, in Mr Crankly's kitchen.

'Hello. I just came to, um…'

'You came for him,' Mr Crankly said, nodding towards Monty.

Patrick nodded meekly.

Monty was busy pushing his tongue around the tin of

condensed milk. 'Scrumdiddilydoo,' he said, to no one in particular.

Mr Crankly stood and moved past Patrick to the fridge where he took out another beer and a large bottle of lemonade.

'Had to fix him up,' Mr Crankly said.

It was then Patrick noticed Monty had a bit of gauze bandage wrapped around one of his paws.

'What happened?' Patrick asked.

'He put a paw through the greenhouse window,' Mr Crankly replied, opening his second beer.

Patrick moved further into the kitchen, still a little cautious. Was this a trap? 'It's awfully nice of you, I mean—'

Mr Crankly coughed, interrupting Patrick. 'I never leave a fallen man behind.'

'It's just a scratch, chaps,' Monty said, helpfully.

'You mean you haven't called the

authorities?' Patrick wanted to be absolutely sure Mr Crankly wasn't waiting for the police and a trained shooter to turn up. He didn't think Mr Crankly would have bothered to wrap Monty's paw and invited him to play chess but you never knew with people.

'No,' Mr Crankly said. 'I haven't had this good a game in years.' He gestured to the chess board. 'I was right though – you were up to something. So this is your little secret, eh?'

'Not such a little secret,' Patrick said, thinking about how huge Monty looked in Mr Crankly's small kitchen.

The corners of Mr Crankly's mouth moved upwards. 'Heh,' he said.

Patrick wasn't a hundred percent sure but he thought Mr Crankly had made an attempt at a chuckle.

Patrick turned to Monty. 'I thought you'd gone because of what I said to you.'

Monty looked up at Patrick and smiled. 'All forgotten, old chum.'

Patrick felt relieved. He watched as Mr Crankly took a glass from the cupboard, filled it with lemonade then handed it to him.

'There's ginger biscuits in the tin. Help yourself.' He pointed to a round, striped biscuit tin on the shiny, polished worktop.

'Thank you.' Patrick took a gulp of the lemonade. His mouth was bone dry. He could still feel his heart beating.

'So he's been staying with you then,' Mr Crankly said, as though Monty were a second cousin living in the spare bedroom.

'His ice raft melted. He fell into the sea and—'

'Yes, he's already briefed me,' Mr Crankly interrupted Patrick.

'An unplanned expedition,' Monty explained from the table where he was slurping the last of the milk.

264

'We've got to get him to a safer territory,' Mr Crankly said. 'It's an emergency evac situation.'

'Yes,' Patrick agreed. He was very relieved to hear this. 'I just don't know how. I've been so worried about it.'

Mr Crankly straightened his back. 'We need a tactical operation.'

'Do you mean a plan? Patrick asked.

'Oh, gentleman, *please*,' said Monty, pushing the empty tin to one side. 'There really is no need to get your pantaloons in a tangle. All these Fred McMurrays. They aren't good for the nerves. I find worrying to be a truly unnecessary occupation. You begin with a little fret here and there and next thing you know your hands are shaking as you bring the vicar his tea and you haven't drawn the curtains since Thursday. *I,* on the other hand, happen to have had a plan all along.'

28

Both Patrick and Mr Crankly looked at Monty.

'What plan?' Patrick asked.

Monty leaned back on his stool causing it to make a horrible creaking noise. 'Well, I arrived here *one way*, did I not?'

Patrick nodded and Mr Crankly made a grunting noise.

'Therefore,' Monty continued, 'I shall return *the same way*.'

Patrick didn't think much of Monty's plan. 'It's too risky,' he told Monty. 'You were incredibly lucky not to be seen on the

way here. You can't expect to be so lucky again.'

'Oh, but I *can*,' Monty said. 'Luck, dear boy, runs freely through my veins. I have always been a lucky bear. And look at how wonderfully fortunate I have been in meeting you fine fellows.'

At this, Patrick blushed a little.

'Besides, it isn't only luck but stealth, dexterity, fleet-footedness, and a learned and matured cognition, that led to my safe arrival. Quite frankly,' Monty said, tapping the claw of his injured paw against his temple, 'I used my noggin.'

Patrick looked to Mr Crankly hoping he would realise how ridiculous this idea was but Mr Crankly seemed to be considering what Monty was saying.

'You reckon you could get to the Thames without being seen?' Mr Crankly asked.

'Oh, certainly,' Monty replied. 'I can swim

for almost two minutes underwater without surfacing. When I do, I shall rise slowly, like a submarine, ears first, take a discreet breath, then off I'll go again. I can swim at a rate of six point two miles per hour.'

Patrick turned to Mr Crankly. 'How far is the Thames from here?'

Mr Crankly was leaning against the sink thinking. 'About fifty miles,' he said.

Patrick tried to work this out. It was like one of Mr Carson's Maths questions.

If a polar bear swimming at six point two miles per hour had to get from Hertfordshire to the River Thames in central London, a distance of approximately fifty miles, how long would it take the polar bear?

Patrick had never been *that* good at Maths. 'Five hours,' Mr Crankly said. 'Just over.'

Five hours! This seemed to Patrick like a very long time to be swimming along a canal.

'He'd have to go after dark, of course,' Mr

Crankly said. 'He'd want to be arriving at the docks by dawn.' Mr Crankly nodded towards Monty. 'You'll be able to catch a boat then.'

'Perfectly doable. I've been saving my energy for the journey. And I've been well catered for, thanks to your generous hospitality.' Monty lifted the condensed milk tin to his eye and peered inside it. He frowned. 'Speaking of which – I don't suppose I could trouble you, old chum, for a little snack?'

'He's always hungry,' Patrick whispered to Mr Crankly.

'It's the sea ice melting,' Mr Crankly said gruffly, handing Monty another tin of condensed milk. 'Not so many ringed seals for the polar bears to eat. I saw it on a documentary. It's a particular interest of mine. It means polar bears are roaming further than they used to. Although Hertfordshire must be a record.'

Monty grinned proudly.

Mr Crankly went to his fridge then handed Monty a packet of fresh kippers. 'Here, you can have these too.'

'Oh, marvellous!' Monty opened the packet and tipped the orange fish into his open mouth.

Patrick watched Monty's sharp teeth chewing up the fish.

Monty burped loudly. 'Pardon me.'

'I love kippers,' Mr Crankly said. 'I have them for breakfast on Sundays. Susan used to make me cook them outside on my old army stove, even in the winter. She didn't like the smell.' Mr Crankly chuckled to himself.

Patrick wasn't sure they had time to be talking about kippers. He turned to Monty. 'But what if you get lost?' he asked. 'How will you know which way is London?'

'Oh, that's easy,' Monty said. 'I'll just follow my nose. London has a very distinct smell: unwashed socks, river weed, coffee, hummus,

fox corpse and an undertone of lavender: a heady blend of opulence and poverty.'

'I see,' Patrick said. But then he thought of something else.

'How will you know which boat to stow away on? I mean, what if you get on a boat that's going *the wrong way*. You could end up in the Bahamas. How will you know the boat you board will be passing Greenland?'

'The Bahamas,' Monty said thoughtfully. 'That could be interesting. I'd better hang on to the sunglasses.'

Mr Crankly looked thoughtful. 'Most boats from the Thames will be going across to Europe. Probably a fair few will go up to the North Sea and the Netherlands.'

'Oh, splendid,' Monty said. 'Uncle Cecil's in Norway. Anyhow, I shall speak with the river trout before I board a boat. Those eagle-eyed fish know all the comings and goings of the Thames.'

'The most tricky part of the operation will be getting him from here to the canal,' said Mr Crankly. 'I'm surprised he wasn't seen when he made his way from there to your garage.'

'Luck is in my veins,' Monty said, prodding his chest with a claw.

'I'll bring a van,' Mr Crankly said. 'I can back the van up against your garage and Monty can climb in. We can take him part of the way. I know a quiet part of the canal. Susan and I used to sit there and look for the kingfisher. It's about five miles from here. It will save some swimming time.'

'Ooh, a road trip,' Monty said.

'We'll park next to the canal and open the doors. Monty can slip into the water and get away.' Mr Crankly seemed almost excited by the plan.

Patrick was still surprised Mr Crankly was

272

being so kind and helpful. 'Are you sure you don't mind bringing a van?'

Mr Crankly made a grunting noise. 'I've still got contacts. An old chum of mine has a three tonner.' He looked at Monty. 'Should be plenty. He's a no-questions-asked man. Totally trustworthy. And of course I don't mind. It's not every day you get to be involved in an operation like this, Pipsqueak. It's a rescue mission.'

'It's Patrick,' Patrick said, but Mr Crankly only sniffed and reached for a Fisherman's Friend from his top pocket.

'I guess it is a rescue mission,' Patrick said quietly. 'If he stays he'll end up being captured, won't he?'

They both looked at Monty who was busy licking the kipper packet.

'Or worse,' Mr Crankly said, under his breath.

'When shall we do this?'

'Wednesday night. Midnight,' Mr Crankly replied. 'I'll check the port departures on the internet. There's bound to be a boat or two Monty could catch.' He glanced at Monty. 'Just in case the river trout are unsure.'

'Splendid,' Monty said.

Patrick shook his head. 'My dad will be back tomorrow afternoon. He might go in the garage.'

Mr Crankly grunted. 'Keep him out of it. Distract him.'

'Can't we make it tonight instead?'

'No, I'm going to a flower-arranging group tonight. I'm giving a talk on roses.'

'Oh, roses. How exciting!' Monty said.

'What about tomorrow then?' Patrick asked.

'I'm busy tomorrow.'

'Doing what?'

'Keep your nose out of it, Pipsqueak. We'll go Wednesday.'

274

Patrick sighed. He looked at the clock on Mr Crankly's kitchen wall. He'd better be getting back in case his mum woke up. He was supposed to be making himself beans on toast and here he was planning a rescue mission.

He noticed that next to his clock, Mr Crankly had a tea towel of a map hung on the wall. It was a map of some islands and it said *The Falklands Campaign*. That was the war Mr Crankly had fought in. Falklands, not Forklands!

'You'll have to take him with you for now,' Mr Crankly said, looking at Monty. 'I'd keep him here in the kitchen but he's a bit fragrant.' Mr Crankly wrinkled his nose.

'I had noticed,' Patrick said.

'I can hear you, you know,' Monty said loudly. 'I can assure you the ladies go wild for a bit of *eau de Monty*.'

'He can stay until it gets dark though,' Mr

Crankly said. 'I'll see him safely through the fence. I'd put him in my garage but I've got my Triumph Spitfire in there.'

'You've got a Spitfire?'

'Triumph Spitfire. Nineteen sixty-six. Mark two. British racing green. Concours condition, she is. Those claws are going nowhere near her.' Mr Crankly glanced at Monty.

'Well, thank you,' Patrick said, feeling grateful he at least didn't have to get Monty back to the garage right now.

'Besides,' Mr Crankly said, 'we need to play another game. Best of three, I should think.'

'Quite right,' Monty said. 'I can't be seen to lose to a human being. Whatever will I tell the narwhals?'

Patrick followed Mr Crankly along the hallway and into the living room. He stopped in front of the mantelpiece. 'Is this you?' he asked, looking at the photograph of the wedding couple.

'Yes,' Mr Crankly said. 'That's me alright.'

Patrick peered closely at the photograph. The man *did* look like Mr Crankly, only younger, and happy.

'And that's my Susan,' Mr Crankly said, moving closer to the photograph.

Patrick looked at the woman in the wedding dress holding flowers. She was very pretty. He knew Mr Crankly's wife had died some years ago. Patrick thought he had a vague memory of her from when he was much younger: a woman in a long dress watering the roses in the front garden and waving to him as he passed by in his buggy with his mum and Mr Nutkins.

'Best thing I ever did,' Mr Crankly said gruffly, 'asking my Susan to marry me. They don't come much better than her, Pipsqueak. I'll tell you that.'

Patrick noticed that even though Mr

Crankly still sounded like Mr Crankly, his voice had softened a little.

Patrick thought of his own parents and his dad being nervous around his mum because she was *beautiful, and intelligent,* and he didn't think he had a chance with her.

'Were you nervous around Mrs Crankly, when you first met her, I mean?'

Mr Crankly looked at Patrick and chuckled a little. 'As hell,' he said. He turned and walked towards the conservatory doors, holding one open for Patrick.

'Thanks,' Patrick said, looking towards the garden. 'I'd best get home to my mum.'

Mr Crankly straightened his back. 'I'll see you Wednesday, Private Jolly. Here. Midnight. Don't be late.'

'I won't be,' Patrick said, thinking that 'Private Jolly', was at least a progression from 'Pipsqueak'.

It wasn't until he was making his way

278

across the dark garden that he remembered he had the big fight with Jake tomorrow. Who knew what would happen after school? He might be in hospital. Or dead. He might not be able to make Wednesday because the surgeons would still be sewing all the pieces of him back together, stitching his arms and legs back on.

Patrick thought that Mr Crankly wasn't so bad at all, one you got to know him. He was just sad, like Patrick's mum, only it made Mr Crankly grumpy, rather than tired.

Patrick knew the next two days were going to be hard and that he had to be brave, not just for his fight tomorrow, but for Monty who needed his help to get home, and for his mum, and for Mr Crankly. Sometimes, Patrick thought, you had to put other people, or polar bears, before yourself. That was just the way it was.

29

The following morning, Patrick walked to school slowly, dreading the day ahead. It was a sunny day, bright and cold, but the sun didn't make him feel any better. His body felt heavy, and kind of floppy, like he was a wooden puppet with no strings. He was miserable about the prospect of being beaten up by Jake. He needed to be fit enough to help Monty. This would be difficult with broken arms and legs.

What happened today after school with Jake could affect the rest of his time at secondary school. Kids would probably still

be talking about the way he got 'smashed up' by Jake when they were in Year Ten. He'd be known forever as 'smashed up boy'. He'd have to move schools and get up *a whole hour* earlier to go to another school on the other side of town which was so far away the kids probably had different accents. He'd have to sit on the bus in the mornings with all the old ladies and their shopping trollies. He'd probably never see Sammy again (even though Sammy hated him). Another friend gone, just like Tommy. Maybe he wasn't supposed to have friends. He'd probably never see Lily again either who was always so nice to him despite being related to a Neanderthal.

Everyone at school was talking about the fight. Even a couple of Year Eight boys sidled up to Patrick at break time and asked him if he was the kid who was having the fight with Jake Sutherland later. They looked him up and down. One of them said, *take bets at*

500/1 whilst the other one wrote something down in a notepad.

The end of the day came around much more quickly than Patrick would have liked. The school was eerily quiet. He grabbed his rucksack and made his way reluctantly out of the doors and across the playground. The sun had disappeared a few hours ago and now the sky was full of grey clouds. Perhaps, he thought, no one would be there after all. His fight with Jake would be one of those rumours that never came to anything. Maybe Jake's warning in the P.E. changing rooms had been just all talk.

When he looked towards the top field, he could see this wasn't the case. It looked like half the school had turned up.

As he approached, someone called out, 'There he is!'

The crowd moved aside for him and Patrick saw Jake standing in a clearing in the middle

talking to Caleb. When Caleb saw Patrick he stepped backwards, giving Jake room. Jake turned and looked at him. He didn't even smile his Bruce the shark smile, he just stood there glaring at Patrick. He looked ready for a fight.

Patrick put his rucksack on the ground. As he did so he caught sight of a square of yellow stripy sock.

He looked up and caught Sammy's eye. Sammy didn't look angry with him anymore, only worried. Sammy shook his head as if to say, *you don't have to go through with this, man.*

He turned away from Sammy. He felt bad knowing Sammy was still on his side, despite how horrible he'd been to him.

'Fight, fight!' someone was chanting. The crowd joined in. 'Fight, fight!'

Patrick watched as Jake clenched his fist. Jake's face was set in a hard, mean expression.

Patrick knew Jake wouldn't stop until he'd won, until Patrick was just a sticky, bony blob mashed into the mud. He waited for Jake to throw the first punch. If Patrick got one in before Jake it would only make Jake more enraged.

The crowd had formed a tight circle around Jake and Patrick. Everyone was ready.

Jake took a step towards Patrick, his fist still clenched.

'Jake, what the hell do you think you're doing? Stop this right now!'

Patrick turned. His vision was slightly blurred, probably because of all the adrenaline pumping through his veins, but it looked as though the crowd had parted and a princess in a long yellow dress was floating towards him. Patrick thought he must be hallucinating, or perhaps concussed, but then he remembered Jake hadn't actually hit him yet. Or maybe he had. Maybe Patrick was already dead and

an angel was coming towards him. Perhaps angels all looked like princesses.

'Lily, go away,' Jake muttered.

Patrick blinked. The princess in yellow was Lily. She looked furious. She was stomping towards them, holding her dress up to stop it from getting muddy. She was wearing little glittery shoes.

'One of the teacups told me,' Lily said. 'I was hoping it couldn't be true. You two, fighting?'

Patrick noticed that the crowd had gone very quiet. This is not what they were expecting – a *very* popular, *very* angry Year Nine girl dressed like a princess arriving on the scene.

'This is between me and Patrick,' Jake said. 'It's none of your business.'

Patrick nodded, although he wasn't sure why.

'None of my *business?*' Lily said, narrowing

her eyes. 'My rehearsal is interrupted because my brother is about to do something stupid he might regret for a very long time – something that could lead to him being *expelled*, and you say it's *none of my business?*'

'It's boy stuff,' Luke chipped in.

Lily whirled around and gave Luke a look that made him instantly stop talking.

'This is ridiculous. You two have lived one street away from each other your whole lives.'

'He's not my friend,' Jake muttered.

'I don't *care*,' Lily said, folding her arms across her chest. 'Who started it?'

Jake shrugged whilst Luke and Caleb looked at their shoes.

Sammy stepped forward. 'Excuse me Belle, um, Lily.' Sammy blushed then cleared his throat. 'Jake, Luke and Caleb have been bullying Patrick for weeks. I've seen it. They trip him up and call him names. They even put him on a peg.'

Patrick stared at Sammy. Why was he saying all this, embarrassing him in front of everyone?

Lily studied Sammy carefully. She looked at his socks and frowned. She turned to Patrick. 'Is this true, Patrick?'

Patrick could feel his cheeks turning red. 'Yes,' he said quietly.

Lily shook her head. She looked disgusted. Patrick couldn't tell if it was because of Jake, or him, or Sammy's socks.

'Look, Lily, why don't you go back to the hall and let me and Patrick have this out.' Jake was angry now. 'And I'll deal with you later, Sammy.'

Lily glared at her brother. 'I don't think so, Jake Reginald Sutherland.'

Someone in the crowd sniggered.

'It was my great-grandad's name,' Jake mumbled.

'I know you're angry because Mum and

Dad are getting divorced,' Lily said to Jake, 'but we're not the only ones with problems. Making someone else feel bad because you feel bad, isn't okay, Jake. You know Patrick's sister died?'

Jake was staring at his shoes. He said nothing.

Patrick felt a lump rise in his throat at the mention of Evie-Ann. He heard some gasps from the crowd and someone whisper, *I didn't know that.*

Lily was still staring at Jake. 'What do you think Mum's going to say when she gets a call to say you've been fighting? How's that going to help anything?'

Jake shrugged but his lip was trembling. He sniffed and wiped a tear from his eye with the sleeve of his blazer. 'Got a cold,' he muttered.

'Go,' Lily told Jake. 'I'm not leaving until you do.'

'Fine,' Jake said, sniffing and reaching

for his rucksack. 'I would have beaten him anyway.'

The crowd began to disperse. Patrick watched Sammy walk away with Gavin and Arnav. Jake, Luke and Caleb were walking towards the gate, their heads down.

Lily turned to Patrick. 'Are you okay?' she asked.

Patrick nodded. He seemed to have lost the power of speech. He thought if he tried to talk, he might cry.

Lily came over and put her arm around him. 'He won't bother you again. He'll have me to do deal with if he does.'

'Thanks,' Patrick was trying *really* hard not to cry now. He didn't even know why he felt like this. He hadn't been hurt at all.

Lily kissed Patrick on the cheek then stepped away. 'I've got to get back to rehearsals. Will you be alright?'

Patrick nodded. 'I'll be fine.'

'I know you will be.'

Patrick watched Lily gather up the bottom of her dress and make her way across the grass towards the playground.

He stood alone with his rucksack in an empty field. Above him, the clouds were gathering. It looked like it was going to rain. It was all over. He wasn't going to get beaten up and Jake was going to stop being mean to him.

He thought of something else.

Lily Sutherland just kissed me!

30

When he got home from school he realised his mum had tidied the house a little during the day, which was a good sign. She'd even organised a Sainsbury's delivery and told Patrick she was going to make them all a Thai curry for tea. This was another good sign. Patrick's dad loved curry. You wouldn't try to make the house nice and cook someone their favourite meal if you were going to split up, would you? Patrick hoped it wasn't just his mum trying to pretend that everything was okay for *his* sake.

At six o'clock, Patrick heard his dad's car in the driveway. He'd recognise that rattle anywhere. He raced downstairs and opened the front door. His dad was lifting his bags out of the boot. He was wearing his old green woolly jumper and his beard needed a trim. Patrick ran to him and gave him a big hug, there on the driveway, not caring who saw. His dad ruffled Patrick's hair.

'Hey, kiddo. I've missed you.' He squeezed Patrick tightly then glanced up at the house. 'Thanks for holding the fort.'

'No problem,' Patrick said, as if the week had been a breeze. 'I've missed you too.'

'Anything much happen around here?' his dad asked, closing the boot of the car.

'Nah,' Patrick said, smiling to himself. 'It's been a quiet week.'

'How's your mum?'

'Okay,' Patrick said. 'Kind of. I think,' he added.

Patrick's dad nodded like he knew what Patrick meant.

'She's making Thai curry.'

'Oh,' his dad said. 'That's good.'

'She painted half a wall.'

His dad raised an eyebrow. 'Intriguing.'

Patrick followed his dad inside the house. In the kitchen, he watched as his mum and dad hugged. They even kissed on the lips, which was *definitely* a good sign.

'It smells delicious in here,' his dad said, which made his mum smile. 'You didn't have to cook,' he added.

His mum only shrugged and reached for the rice. 'I guess I wanted to.'

'You had Thai food on your first date,' Patrick reminded his parents.

Patrick's dad squeezed Patrick's shoulder then glanced at Patrick's mum. 'So we did.'

Patrick's mum smiled. 'Of course,' she said, 'that's *exactly* why I decided to make it.'

This made them all laugh because it was clear that his mum hadn't really thought of it at all.

'Well, I'd better go unpack,' Patrick's dad said. 'Maybe I've got time for a quick shower?'

'Dinner will be twenty minutes,' his mum replied.

'I've got a bag of outdoor gear to go in the garage,' Patrick's dad said. 'I'll put that away first. Get it out of the hallway so no one trips over it.'

'I'll put it in the garage!' Patrick said, a little too enthusiastically.

'No, it's too heavy. I'll do it.'

'I've been working out.'

Patrick's dad glanced at Patrick's mum who nodded.

'Okay, then, Hercules. Stick it next to the old cameras.'

'If you're still in a helpful mood, after

294

you've done that you can lay the table,' his mum said.

Patrick sighed. He didn't like laying the table. Never mind. At least he had managed to keep his dad out of the garage. They were so close now, to getting Monty home.

Once Patrick's dad had gone upstairs for a shower, Patrick heaved the rucksack from the hallway and dragged it out of the back door.

Monty was in the freezer with *The Complete Works of William Shakespeare*. He was now on the last volume.

'Good evening, old bean. What fine weather we've had today. It's positively tropical out there.'

Patrick couldn't say he agreed with Monty. He thought it was pretty cold. It was still January after all. There was talk of snow this weekend. Mr Carson had mentioned it in Maths yesterday. *With any luck we'll be closed on Monday,* he'd said, looking hopefully across the heads of his Year Seven class and out of the window. And how could Monty tell what the weather was like from inside the garage anyway?

It was then he noticed the picnic basket. It was lined with red gingham and contained several tins of anchovies, pilchards and spam. There was a bottle of ginger beer, a packet of Digestives, a jar of rhubarb jam, two tins of condensed milk and a Baxter's Cream of Chicken soup.

'From Clifford,' Monty said. 'Most generous.'

'Clifford?'

'Clifford Crankly. A hamper,' Monty explained. 'To see me through until

tomorrow, so you don't have to worry, old sport.'

Patrick smiled. It *was* generous of Mr Crankly to give Monty the food. He was glad he wouldn't have to wash any more cars.

'Although I don't much care for the fizzy stuff. It makes my rear end pop. And rather loudly too.'

Patrick grinned. But then he imagined Monty 'popping' tomorrow night as he swam, sending eruptions through the water that were sure to scare away any river trout that might offer directions or boat times.

'Perhaps lay off the ginger beer then.'

'What happened with the fisticuffs?' Monty asked, putting his book down.

'I was saved by a princess.'

Monty shook his head. 'What drama you human beings create. Always getting muddled up in yourselves. And shouldn't it have been the other way around. Shouldn't you have saved the princess?'

Patrick shrugged. 'I don't know. I guess. It's a changing society.' He grinned then put his more serious voice on. 'Now, remember, Monty, my dad's home. You need to be quiet and stay in here. I'll do my best to keep him out of the garage.'

'Got it, old sport. I'll keep my head down.'

'And don't tell anyone about our plan tomorrow night.'

As Patrick said this he wondered if there was anyone Monty *could* tell. Still, it was better to be safe than sorry.

'Mum's the word,' Monty said.

Patrick paused in the doorway. 'Aren't you scared about tomorrow night?' he asked.

'Oh, no,' Monty chuckled. 'There is no point being frightened about something which *might* happen. There will only be what *does* happen, and seeing as I'm not there yet,

I have no cause to be frightened. Besides,' Monty continued, 'as Mr Wilde once said: an idea that is not dangerous is unworthy of being called an idea at all.'

Patrick smiled. He was going miss Monty and his quotes.

31

Patrick was sitting at the kitchen table, half-way through eating his curry, when he heard the sirens. They all heard them. At first the sirens sounded far away but then they began to grow louder. Too loud.

'I wonder what's going on,' his dad said.

Patrick's mum put her fork down and Patrick's dad was already getting up. They all looked at each other, confused.

'It sounds really close,' his mum murmured.

Patrick and his mum followed his dad into the living room where he drew back the curtains. The evening sky flashed blue and

red as the ambulance stopped on the street right outside the house.

'I wonder who it's for,' his mum whispered.

They watched as two paramedics got out of the ambulance, one carrying a large bag. They walked up Mr Crankly's driveway. Patrick and his parents could no longer see the paramedics. They had gone into Mr Crankly's house.

Patrick's dad turned away from the window. 'Oh, dear…'

Patrick felt a strange lurching in his stomach. His legs had gone wobbly. 'Should we go out there?'

He watched as his parents exchanged glances.

'It might be best not to interfere,' Patrick's mum said.

'There's probably not a lot we can do,' Patrick's dad added, although he looked as worried as Patrick's mum.

Across the road, they could see Mrs Wilkinson coming out of number five, wearing a flowery apron and wellies, and with baby Florence on her hip. She reached the end of her driveway then hurried over the road, heading towards them.

The paramedics came out of Mr Crankly's house and Patrick and his parents watched as they opened the back of the ambulance, took out a stretcher, then went back inside.

Patrick didn't wait any longer. He rushed into the hallway, opened the front door and ran out into the driveway. He wanted to do something to help, something to make things better, only he didn't know what to do.

Mrs Wilkinson was coming towards him. 'Hello, love,' she said, softly.

'What's going on?'

'I don't know, love. I came to see.'

'Should we go inside?' Patrick looked towards Mr Crankly's open front door.

Patrick's parents had followed him onto the driveway. He felt his dad's hand on his shoulder. 'We should let them do their work, Patrick.'

The paramedics appeared again. This time they were carrying Mr Crankly out of his front door on the stretcher. Mr Crankly had a blanket over him. His eyes were closed and he was wearing an oxygen mask. Patrick willed Mr Crankly to open his eyes and give him some sort of sign that everything was okay, but he didn't. He didn't open his eyes at all.

Once Mr Crankly was in the ambulance, Mrs Wilkinson went over to the paramedics. They spoke to her quickly in low, hushed voices before climbing into the cab. Patrick couldn't hear what they were saying. The doors closed, the engine started, and then the ambulance was disappearing out of Cherry Tree Close.

'It's his heart,' Mrs Wilkinson said, crossing the driveway.

Patrick swallowed hard. Tommy's grandfather had died from a heart attack. That was why they'd moved to Bristol. To be closer to Tommy's nan.

Patrick looked at his mum. He knew she was thinking of this too because she touched Patrick's other shoulder and said, 'There are different kinds of heart problems. Some can be more serious than others.'

Mrs Wilkinson was nodding. 'Apparently, he began to feel a bit funny. He called the ambulance himself, but when they found him, he was on the floor next to his chair.'

Patrick's dad turned to Patrick. 'I think it's time we all went back inside.'

Patrick looked at his parents and then at Mr Crankly's house. 'But how will we know he's okay!'

'I'll call the hospital tomorrow,' Mrs Wilkinson said. 'I'm sure they'll speak to me.'

'Doesn't he have any family?' Patrick's mum asked, her hand still on Patrick's shoulder.

Mrs Wilkinson shook her head. 'A younger brother in Australia. That's all, as far as I know. It was always just him and Susan. Such an awful thing to happen. Today of all days.'

Patrick and his parents looked blank.

'It's the anniversary of her passing,' Mrs Wilkinson explained, her voice almost a whisper, as if she didn't want to upset baby Florence. 'I saw him this afternoon, buying flowers in the Co-op to take up to the churchyard. He always finds this day difficult, of course.'

Patrick felt a lump forming in his throat. So that was why Mr Crankly hadn't wanted to borrow the van and send Monty home today, why he'd wanted to wait until tomorrow. He'd wanted to be with his wife, to remember her.

He thought of the photograph of Mr and Mrs Crankly on the mantelpiece looking young and happy. He thought of Mr Crankly in his kitchen, finding kippers for Monty, wrapping up Monty's paw, making him a hamper with ginger beer. He thought of the way Mr Crankly always kept his Fisherman's Friend mints in the top pocket of his shirt, and how his voice was gruff but his heart was kind.

He turned and ran inside the house.

32

Patrick lay face down on his bed sobbing. They were the kind of sobs that made your chest feel tight, your body shake, and created a wet patch on your duvet cover. It wasn't fair that Mr Crankly had something wrong with his heart and that Evie-Ann had died right after she had been born.

Patrick cried because Sammy wasn't speaking to him and Monty would never get home. He cried because his mum was sad, his dad might leave, and if that happened he'd have to move away from Cherry Tree Close and his house and bedroom forever.

Patrick heard his door open and quiet footsteps. He looked up and found his mum and dad sitting on the end of his bed.

'I'm sorry,' his mum said softly.

Patrick's dad looked concerned. 'We didn't realise you knew him that well.'

'I guess he *has* lived here all your life,' Patrick's mum said.

Patrick's face was still mostly buried in his duvet and his words sounded muffled. 'His name is Clifford and he isn't as mean as everyone thinks. He's got a tea towel about the war he was in, and he eats kippers for breakfast on Sundays.'

Patrick's parents exchanged glances.

'I didn't realise you'd even been in his house,' his mum said, looking a little worried.

'It was the other day,' Patrick said. 'I… dropped a package round.' Patrick hated lying and having to do it caused another loud sob to escape his throat.

Patrick's mum put her hand on his arm. 'He'll be well looked after by the doctors and nurses.'

Patrick knew this but it didn't help much. He managed to sit up then wiped his eyes and hugged his knees to his chest. 'You guys need to start telling me the truth.'

Patrick's mum and dad looked at each other, and then at Patrick.

'The truth about what?' Patrick's mum asked, confused.

'The truth about what's going on,' Patrick said. 'About whether you're getting a divorce or not.'

Patrick's parents both looked surprised but Patrick wasn't falling for it. Things had been wrong for such a long time and he wasn't going to be lied to any longer.

'I know dad *wanted* to go away – it wasn't just for the money. I know it.'

To Patrick's surprise, his dad nodded. 'You're

right,' he said. 'You do deserve to know the truth.'

'I'm not a little kid anymore. I'm at *senior* school now.'

'That's true,' Patrick's dad said. 'And the truth is, I did need to go away because it was a good job, but I also wanted to.'

Patrick had a horrible feeling in his stomach but he had asked for the truth and he intended to handle it.

'Things have been pretty tough since Evie-Ann died,' Patrick's dad continued.

Patrick's mum had been staring at Patrick's duvet cover but she looked up at the mention of Evie-Ann. Patrick's dad hadn't said Evie-Ann's name for a long time, not since she'd died.

'It's hard looking after someone who's very sad, especially when you feel pretty sad yourself.' Patrick's dad coughed, clearing his

310

throat, but Patrick could see his dad's eyes had grown wet.

Patrick's mum took hold of Patrick's dad's hand and squeezed it.

'I was feeling low and I *was* looking forward to spending some time by myself. It was nice at first but the truth is I missed you guys.'

Patrick frowned. 'Really?' he asked.

'Of course!' his dad said. 'I kept thinking how cool it would be if you were there. You could have helped me make the fire. We'd have played Cluedo and roasted chestnuts and built a snowman. And you could have helped by coming out with me and bringing your binoculars.'

'And Mum too?' Patrick asked, wanting to make sure. 'You missed Mum too?'

Patrick's dad looked at Patrick's mum and squeezed her hand again.

'Mum too,' he said. 'We're not getting a

divorce, Patrick. At least, that's not what I want.'

'It's not what I want either,' Patrick's mum whispered.

Patrick was so relieved but he also knew his mum was still sad and that it was his fault. As soon as he remembered this, he began to cry again.

'It's all my fault,' he said, between sobs.

'Patrick, what are you talking about?' his mum asked.

'I never wanted a sister,' Patrick said. 'Not at first. I wished it could be just the three of us and now it is and it's *horrible*. Now I wish she could be here but it's too late.' Now that he'd started sobbing again he couldn't stop.

His mum was crying a little bit too.

Patrick's dad reached for Patrick and put his arm around him. He still had hold of Patrick's mum's hand.

'Hey,' he said. 'There's something else that

everyone in this family needs to realise.' He looked at Patrick and then at Patrick's mum. 'Evie-Ann dying was *no one's* fault, not yours, not your mum's and not mine.'

Patrick's sobs subsided and his mum wiped her eyes with the sleeve of her jumper. 'Patrick,' she said. 'It wasn't your fault.'

Patrick looked from his mum to his dad. Maybe they were right. He could see they didn't blame him even though he'd blamed himself for such a long time.

'I just want things to be normal,' he whispered.

'I know,' Patrick's mum said. 'And that isn't too much to ask. I'll never not be sad about Evie-Ann dying, Patrick, but I *am* getting a little better each day. I'm beginning to accept things as they are and allowing time to pass. I am learning that I can be happy even though I'm sad.'

Patrick leaned against his headboard. 'But

isn't that just pretending? I don't want you to just pretend that everything's okay.'

'No,' Patrick's mum said. 'It isn't pretending. You can be sad about something but still be happy and grateful for the other wonderful things that you *do* have.' She looked at Patrick and his dad.

Patrick nodded. 'Thanks, Mum. That makes sense.' Patrick knew his mum was telling the truth. 'I feel so bad about Mr Crankly,' he whispered.

'I know.' His mum leaned over and kissed the top of Patrick's head. 'Let's see what we can find out tomorrow.'

'If no one knows anything,' Patrick's dad said, 'then we'll call the hospital ourselves. I promise.'

'Thanks,' Patrick said. 'I'd really appreciate that.'

It was then Patrick noticed Mr Nutkins. He'd been so busy crying that he hadn't

even seen him sitting up on his bed with his head sewn back on. He looked like he'd been through the washing machine.

'You fixed him?'

'Yes,' his mum said. 'I found him in your wastepaper basket. I sewed him up. He's been with you a long time.'

Patrick hugged his mum. His dad joined in too, wrapping his arms around them. Patrick reached for Mr Nutkins. It was only fair that he should get in on the family hug too. He was so glad to have them all back.

33

The following morning, at seven AM, Patrick was downstairs in his pyjamas, putting a piece of bread into the toaster, when the doorbell rang.

He left his toast and peered anxiously into the hallway. His mum was coming down the stairs. 'It's okay,' she said. 'I've got it.'

Patrick's dad appeared from the living room and they all went to the door.

Mrs Wilkinson was standing on the doorstep in a pink coat and furry snow boots, even though there was no snow. Patrick knew she had come to tell them something

about Mr Crankly. He felt his chest tighten.

'He's going to be okay,' Mrs Wilkinson said.

Patrick felt the relief flood through him. He could hear his dad exhaling.

'Thank you,' his mum said. She looked at Patrick. 'We've all been very worried.'

'He had heart murmurs,' Mrs Wilkinson explained. They'll need to keep him in for a few days, maybe a week, but then he'll be able to come home. I've just come from the hospital.'

Patrick was so pleased to hear this, he almost felt like hugging Mrs Wilkinson. He turned to his mum. 'Maybe we could get him something?' He thought perhaps Mr Crankly might like some kippers, tinned pilchards or ginger beer to replace what he'd given to Monty.

'Of course,' Patrick's mum said, squeezing Patrick's shoulder.

'I'll bring him some hot dinners when he gets back,' Mrs Wilkinson said. 'Cooking for six won't be much more trouble than cooking for five.'

'That's very kind of you,' Patrick's dad said. 'I'm sure we can help out too.'

'Oh,' Mrs Wilkinson said, 'I almost forgot.' She reached into her pocket and handed Patrick a piece of folded paper. 'He asked me to give this to you.'

'Thank you,' Patrick said, taking the paper. He put it into his pyjama pocket. He had no idea what it was but he wanted to open it alone.

Once Mrs Wilkinson had gone, Patrick raced upstairs, forgetting all about his toast. He flopped down on his bed and took out the piece of paper. It would include instructions of some kind. Mr Crankly might not be around tonight to help get Monty to the canal but

he'd know what Patrick should do. He'd have a back-up plan.

Patrick unfolded the paper. It read:

Dear Private Jolly, I'm promoting you
to Sergeant.
You'll think of something.

Patrick stared at the note. *You'll think of something?* Was that all Mr Crankly had to say? It wasn't at all helpful. In fact, Patrick had no further idea of what to do than he had before Mrs Wilkinson had given him the note. It was completely useless.

He screwed up the note and threw it across the room.

He stared out of the window at the garage, the hammock and Mr Crankly's empty fish pond.

He realised that even though he didn't have

a clue how to get Monty from his garage to the canal at midnight tonight, Mr Crankly had thought he would be able to come up with an idea. Mr Crankly had put his faith in him. Mr Crankly *believed* in him and that had to count for something.

Patrick thought of the long journey Monty had to make to London, and then to Greenland. All Patrick had to do was to get him to the canal without him being seen.

He lay on his bed, staring at the ceiling.

He thought of Monty, and of that first day, when he had seen him dozing in the chest freezer. He thought of how he'd only gone into the garage to put the Christmas decorations away.

Patrick opened his eyes. He sat up and scrambled to the edge of his bed.

That was it!

He knew now, what he had to do tonight.

He'd thought of something, and it might just work.

He also knew there was another thing he had to do today at school first. A *really* important thing. He reached for his uniform and dressed quickly. Perhaps he had time to see if his toast was still there.

Patrick left ten minutes early for school so he could check on Monty. The last thing he wanted was Monty to go wandering off just before he was about to go home.

He needn't have worried. Monty was dozing in the freezer as usual. He did seem to sleep a lot. Patrick wondered if he was hibernating. It was winter after all.

First of all he had to tell Monty about Mr Crankly. He shut the garage door softly behind him, causing Monty to open his eyes.

'Listen, Monty. This is really important. Mr Crankly, Clifford I mean, he's in hospital.

He's going to be okay, but we need to move to plan B tonight.'

'Oh, dear! Are you sure he's going to be well again soon, old chap?'

'Quite sure,' Patrick said. 'Mrs Wilkinson — she's another of our neighbours. She's been to see him in hospital.'

Monty nodded thoughtfully. 'Do send him my best wishes. I should have liked to have said cheerio though.'

'I'll tell him for you when he comes home.'

'Make sure you do, old sport. He's a good egg, that one. Those kippers were delicious.'

Monty closed his eyes as if remembering the kippers. He looked sleepy again.

'Monty, shouldn't you be hibernating?' Patrick asked.

Monty opened one eye. 'My dear boy, male polar bears are not deep hibernators, unlike our pregnant female companions. We

merely enter a state of carnivore lethargy. We conserve energy.'

'I see,' Patrick said. 'I guess you're conserving energy for tonight then?'

'I am indeed, old sport. I must say, I can't wait to get back to the ice and catch myself a seal or two.'

Patrick nodded. He didn't really want to think about that. 'Monty, can I ask you something?'

Monty sat up. 'Anything, dear boy. Ask away.'

'Well, you see… I've got this friend from school—'

'A chum? How wonderful!'

'Yes, but we've fallen out.'

'Oh, dear.'

'I want to make it up with him but I really think he hates me.'

Monty considered this. 'I fell out with a

bear once. It was over a rather tasty whale carcass.'

'Did you make it up with him?'

Monty smiled. 'I did indeed. Feeling that, perhaps, I had been a *little* too defensive, I went and found the bear in question and offered him a freshly caught salmon. We've remained chums ever since.'

'Um. Thanks,' Patrick said, wondering how this was going to help him with Sammy. 'I had better get to school, Monty. Don't leave the garage, and I'll see you tonight.'

Monty waved a paw in the air then settled back into the chest freezer. 'It's good to have a friend,' he said.

Patrick was just about to remark that that was *exactly* what his mum had said to him but Monty had already closed his eyes.

34

At school, everything was almost back to normal. Jake, Luke and Caleb looked pretty sheepish. Jake didn't speak to Patrick – that was probably never going to happen – but Caleb asked to borrow a highlighter and then *actually* returned it.

Maybe things were going to be better after all.

Patrick didn't get a chance to speak to Sammy all morning. There just wasn't the right moment. Well, that's what he had been telling himself, but when the bell rang for lunch, he wondered if perhaps there *had* been moments when he *could* have spoken to Sammy, only he hadn't wanted to. Or not that he hadn't *wanted* to, exactly. More, if he was being honest with himself, that he hadn't been quite brave enough.

Patrick saw Sammy over by the lockers. Sammy closed his locker door without noticing him, slung his rucksack over his shoulder and instead of walking out the doors to the playground, headed along the corridor, away from the canteen. Where was he going?

Patrick followed, feeling kind of guilty for following Sammy but knowing he had to speak to him before the end of the day, before too much time passed and they never made up.

Sammy walked past the I.T. suites and into the arts block. He pushed the doors to the drama studio and went inside. Patrick followed.

The drama studio was busy. Students were milling around. Their music teacher, Mr Jennings, was over by the piano. Several pupils with instruments stood next to him. Someone was stacking chairs that had been left out. On the stage, Patrick saw Lily holding her script. She was with a few other Year Nine's who also had scripts. Sammy was adding his rucksack to a pile of bags in the corner when he saw Patrick. He looked surprised but quickly turned away.

Patrick took a deep breath then headed over to him.

'Hey.'

'Oh, hey,' Sammy said.

'What's going on in here?' Patrick asked.

'Play rehearsals.'

'Oh.'

Patrick must have looked confused because Sammy said, 'I signed up. I asked Lily if there were any parts left, or anything I could do.

She spoke to the drama teacher for me. I'm playing villager number eight slash nine. It's not a speaking part or anything. I'm only on stage for a few minutes. My mum wanted me to do something "extra-curricular".' Sammy shrugged. 'I wanted to do it though.'

Patrick nodded. 'Should be fun.'

'Yeah.'

Patrick wasn't sure this was going well but at least Sammy was speaking to him.

'I just wanted to say – thanks for being there for me on the field.'

Sammy shrugged.

'Do you think we could be friends again?'

Sammy sighed. 'Of course. But you got mad at *me*, remember? I never stopped being your friend, I just thought I had better give you some space. You seemed kind of wound up.'

'I know,' Patrick said. 'I'm sorry.'

'I'm sorry too. You've got a lot going on.'

'Yeah, but I shouldn't have taken it out on you.'

'Let's forget it.'

'Really?'

'Yeah, really,' Sammy said. 'As long as *you* still want to be friends with *me*.'

'Of course I do!' Patrick was surprised. Why wouldn't he want to be friends with Sammy?

Sammy was staring at a spot on the floor. 'It's just that you're pretty cool. You know, you're good at football and you've got really cool parents. Your dad and that stoat picture…'

Patrick looked at Sammy in amazement. He never knew Sammy saw him like that. 'Me? Cool? Haven't you noticed the way Jake and the others have been picking on me?'

'Yeah, but they're wombats.'

Patrick smiled then thought of something else. 'And when have you ever seen me sitting at the cool table at lunch?'

Sammy rolled his eyes. 'You don't need to sit at the cool table to be cool. Anyway, *our* table is the cool table. It's got me on it.'

Patrick grinned. 'True. To be honest, I try to just keep myself to myself. Or I did – before all this Jake business started.'

Sammy nodded. 'You know Jake's never going to pick on you again, right?'

Patrick shrugged.

'Seriously.' Sammy glanced over at the stage. 'Lily's on the anti-bullying council. Actually, she *founded* it. She's totally anti-bullying. She had a right go at Jake, and she's going to do a special anti-bullying assembly next week.'

Patrick looked over at Lily who was practicing her ballroom dance with a boy called Toby who was good at rugby and

who was playing The Beast. He had huge shoulders and a thick jaw. He did look kind of beast-like. He wouldn't need much make-up. Patrick was glad Lily was going to do the assembly, even if it was because of him. He turned back to Sammy.

'Thanks for telling Lily on the field yesterday about Jake bullying me. I didn't want her to know at the time, but I'm glad you told her now.'

'It's not on, dude. They shouldn't have been bullying you.'

'I know.' Patrick grinned, thinking of something. 'We did get them into massive trouble though.'

Sammy grinned too. 'I heard Mr Plimmswood had to take his jacket to the dry cleaners. Jake's got to pay the bill.'

One of the Year Nine's on the stage moved to the front. 'Can I have all the villagers, please! Scene two!'

'I'd better go,' Sammy said. 'See you tomorrow?'

'Sure,' Patrick said. 'But can I ask you something first?'

Sammy nodded.

'Why are you villager eight slash nine, not just villager eight *or* nine?'

'Oh. Villager number nine can only make one performance night so on the first night I'm villager number nine and on the second night I come on as villager number eight, then I have to run around the back, put on a moustache and a hat then come back on as villager number nine.'

Patrick smiled. 'That's funny.'

'Villagers!' The Year Nine girl was shouting, getting impatient.

'I'd better go,' Sammy said. 'But I was thinking... Why don't you come over to mine on Saturday.'

'I'd like that. That would be cool.'

'I'll even show you my garage. If you're lucky.'

'Ha. ha.'

'Villagers! Final call! I'm still missing someone!'

'Gotta go.'

Patrick watched as Sammy leapt up onto the stage. He was wearing one orange sock, one green sock again.

'One more thing!' Patrick called after Sammy.

Sammy turned.

'Would you rather have your hand stuck in a jar or your head stuck in a bucket?'

Sammy grinned. 'It's gotta be the hand in jar,' he called out loudly, causing several heads to turn and look at him in confusion. 'I've got two hands.'

'That's what I was thinking,' Patrick called back.

He smiled to himself and watched as

Sammy went and joined the other villagers. He'd made up with Sammy and he hadn't even had to bring him a salmon. Although Sammy *had* said he liked salmon. Still, it would have been weird. Perhaps it was a good thing he didn't take Monty's advice on everything.

35

The alarm on Patrick's phone went off under his pillow. He reached for it immediately, silencing it by swiping quickly across the screen. He'd made the alarm very quiet but even so, he couldn't risk it waking his parents.

He checked the time, *23:55*, five minutes to midnight.

He quickly changed into his tracksuit trousers and a warm jumper. It wasn't right, sneaking out like this, not telling his parents. It was dangerous. He knew that. He reminded himself, he wouldn't be doing this if it wasn't for Monty. He had to admit though, he felt pretty safe with Monty around. It wasn't like anyone was going to mess with him when they saw him with a large polar bear. Not that he'd have Monty around for much longer if all went to plan tonight, but he didn't want to think about that just yet. It was a shame, in a way, that he hadn't been able to bring Monty to school on the day of his fight to scare Jake although, saying that, Lily had been scary enough. She'd probably scare Monty.

He crept downstairs, making sure to avoid the creaky step. He could hear his dad snoring. It was strange being up this late. The house seemed different. Quieter. He was using the torch on his phone as he didn't want to risk switching a light on.

In the hallway, he took his coat from the peg rail, found his trainers and went into the kitchen where he put them on. When he

336

was ready, he let himself out into the garden. There was half a moon hanging in the sky and even a few stars. It was bitterly cold but he didn't feel it too much. His adrenaline must be pumping, keeping him warm, although he could see his breath in front of his face.

He crept down the side of the house and opened the garage door.

Monty was lying on top of the freezer shining a torch over the Shakespeare book. 'I'm on the last page,' he whispered loudly.

Patrick stood silently for a minute whilst Monty continued to read. What could he say? It was so annoying when somebody interrupted your reading, especially just as you'd reached the last page.

Finally, Monty shut the book. 'Not a bad read. Not quite as good as Oscar Wilde though.' He climbed off the freezer and put the book back in the box where he'd found it. He stretched and yawned, showing his teeth.

'Monty, are you ready?' Patrick asked.

'My dear boy, I was born ready.'

'How's your paw?' Patrick asked, noticing that Monty no longer had the bandage.

'Right as rain, old chap. Healing nicely.'

'Good.'

Patrick crossed the garage and stood in front of the shelving. There was the box of Christmas decorations next to the crate of his dad's old photography equipment. Next to that was the camouflage netting his dad used for hiding under when he was watching animals, waiting to photograph them. The netting was brown and green. When you put it over something, that thing just looked like a pile of leaves, or a bush.

Patrick reached for the netting. It was fairly large. His dad sometimes used it to cover his bird-watching tent. He thought it should be big enough to cover a polar bear.

'Monty, you're going to hide under here.

338

I'll join you once we're out of the garage. We'll go slowly and stick to the edge of the pavement. If a car comes along, we'll stop. We'll look like a large bush, that's all.'

'Ooh, a disguise,' Monty said, looking excited.

'Yes, but I'm sorry, you'll have to swim all the way to London. Do you think you'll manage it?'

'Oh, I should think so. Polar bears are excellent long-distance swimmers. We've had to become even better in recent years, what with the ice melting. More open water, you see.'

Patrick nodded, thinking of Mr Eddy's Geography lessons. He unfolded the netting and threw it over Monty, then arranged it so Monty was completely covered.

'Ready?'

'Ready, old bean.'

Patrick opened the garage door and they

went out onto the driveway. He looked up and down Cherry Tree Close. It was dark and silent. There were no lights on in any of the houses.

Monty shuffled out of the garage under the netting.

'You'll have to guide me I'm afraid, old chap. I'm as blind as a proverbial chiroptera.'

'Isn't that a foot doctor?'

Monty chuckled. 'Bat, dear boy. It's Latin.'

Patrick shook his head. They had to get a move on. He couldn't be seen walking along the street after midnight talking to a bush.

He carefully closed the garage door, pushing it back into place, trying to be as quiet as he could, then crept under the netting.

'Hop on,' Monty said, pointing to his back.

'Really?'

Monty nodded. 'Best way, old chap.'

Patrick clambered onto Monty's back. It was a little scary, being on the back of a

large, wild polar bear. Monty's fur was soft and warm. He smelled of bear and kippers. Monty snuffled around under the netting, getting used to it. Patrick pulled a few plastic leaves from the netting so he could see.

They shuffled to the end of the drive and turned onto Cherry Tree Close. They moved along the pavement, behind the cars, keeping close to the garden walls.

'Go slowly,' Patrick whispered, reminding Monty. A fast-moving bush was bound to draw more attention that a slow-moving one.

As they were passing the Wilkinsons' house, there was a loud crash.

Monty stopped. 'Oh, dear,' he said, putting a paw to his mouth.

There was a hissing noise and a very loud meow.

Patrick could see Tinkerbell through the netting. She'd obviously been startled by the large, moving bush. She'd knocked over the

Wilkinsons' recycling box. An empty baked bean tin rolled down the driveway and a light came on in one of the upstairs windows.

Patrick could feel his heart thumping in his chest as they hid behind the Wilkinsons' garden wall.

'Imbecile,' Monty muttered.

Patrick patted Monty's back, reminding him to be quiet.

The front door opened and Patrick could see Mrs Wilkinson's cat face slippers through the netting.

'Tinkerbell? Was that you my little snuggle muffin?'

Mrs Wilkinson took a step onto the driveway and Patrick held his breath. He could hear Monty breathing steadily through his nose. Patrick was sure he could hear his heart beating too, a steady thump, thump. Or perhaps it was Monty's.

'Where are you my little snoochey poo?

I hope you haven't found any micey wices. You know we don't like those... Ah, there you are. Come on now Tinky winky.'

Tinkerbell ran up the driveway, through Mrs Wilkinson's slippered feet, and into the house.

The door closed and, after a few moments, the light went out.

'That was close,' Patrick whispered.

'A feline of little brain,' Monty said.

'Come on,' Patrick said. 'Let's keep moving.'

It had been a close call with Mrs Wilkinson, and Patrick was growing worried. They hadn't even left Cherry Tree Close. Once they finally got onto Windmill Road, there were bound to be cars passing as it was the main road. He reminded himself that this was Monty's only chance of getting home, and that Mr Crankly had put his faith in him. He bit his lip and tried to ignore the fluttery feeling in his stomach.

They passed Mrs Furrows' bungalow on the corner, including all her garden gnomes, then turned onto Windmill Road. There were fewer parked cars and Patrick felt they were more exposed. They shuffled along for a while, Patrick praying they could make it all the way to the canal. There was the sound of an approaching car.

'Stop,' Patrick whispered, tugging gently on Monty's ear.

They stopped and crouched down as low as they could. The car passed them and Patrick could see it was a taxi. He kept expecting the taxi to turn around, to come back and investigate the strange mound on the pavement.

Luckily, it didn't, but how many more cars would come along?

Patrick looked up and, through

the netting, saw Jake's house. He remembered what Lily had said, *You're not the only one with problems.* Patrick felt sorry for Jake. He wondered if they would ever be friends. Probably not, but who knew? They still had four and a half years of being in the same tutor group left to go.

At least, Patrick thought, they understood each other a little better now.

They crept further along the road. It was a long road.

'Delightful evening,' Monty said, a little too loudly. 'Perfect for a dip in the canal.'

'Shhh! We have to be quiet, remember?' Patrick said, clinging to Monty's fur and looking through the netting from left to right.

It was then they heard the sound of a large vehicle approaching them from behind. It seemed to be slowing down. Its headlights were shining on them.

Patrick didn't know what to do. There was no time to think.

They hunkered down, low to the ground. Patrick closed his eyes tightly, hoping the vehicle would pass.

It didn't.

It was definitely pulling over.

Now it was stopping.

They must have been discovered. The authorities had come for Monty.

They heard a door open. Patrick held onto Monty tightly. He wouldn't let them take him. He heard soft footsteps coming towards them.

The camouflage netting was whipped away.

'Ah, gotcha!'

36

Mr Crankly was standing on the pavement holding the corner of the camouflage netting. He was wearing stripy pyjamas, slippers and a faded red dressing gown. Behind him, parked on the curb, was an ambulance.

'I thought someone might be in need of back-up,' he said.

Patrick was so relieved, he could hardly speak.

'I thought we were toast, old bean,' Monty said. 'Jolly nice of you to show up, Clifford, old chum.'

Mr Crankly opened the back doors of the ambulance.

'Come on,' he said. 'Hop in. Before someone sees us.'

Patrick looked around. All the houses were dark and quiet. There was no sound or sign of a car.

'A road trip, after all,' Monty said, shaking the rest of the netting off and ambling towards the open doors.

'You stole an ambulance?' Patrick asked, his voice a low whisper.

'Borrowed,' Mr Crankly corrected him. 'This is an important operation, Private Jolly. I wasn't about to bail on you. I knew you'd be around here somewhere. I almost didn't see you. Great disguise! Luckily, I've got a trained eye.'

'But your heart?' Patrick asked. 'And you said I was *Sergeant* Jolly.' He forgot to whisper this time.

'Acting Sergeant. I'm back on duty now. And don't you worry about me. Plenty of life left in this old ticker yet.' Mr Crankly prodded his chest. 'It's been through worse. Now let's finish this operation.'

Patrick rolled up the camouflage netting then climbed into the back of the ambulance with Monty. He could hear Mr Crankly getting into the front. The engine spluttered into life.

The inside of the ambulance was very bright and clean. There was a stretcher which Monty sprawled himself onto and a chair that Patrick sat in.

'I've never been in an automobile before,' Monty said, cheerfully.

Patrick hoped Mr Crankly wouldn't make any sharp turns. He didn't fancy being squashed under Monty's weight if he rolled off the stretcher. Carrying a polar bear in an ambulance was bound to be against some kind of health and safety procedure.

'This unplanned adventure calls for "The Song of the Open Road",' Monty announced.

'I'm not sure I like car singing much,' Patrick said, remembering his dad singing along to that Neil Young CD all the way to Dorset to visit Aunt Pru last summer. His mum had joined in with the singing too. No one should have to listen to their parents singing, especially not together.

Monty ignored him and began his song – which turned out not to be a song but, unsurprisingly, a poem.

'Afoot and light-hearted I take to the open road,
Healthy, free, the world before me,
The long brown path before me leading wherever I choose…'

He carried on like this for quite some time. The poem was rather a long one.

'Walt Whitman,' Monty said, when he had finally finished. 'One of America's most significant 19th century poets. A huge inspiration to a distant brown bear relative of mine: great, great uncle Jim–Bob, an early explorer of the frontier, nonetheless.'

Were there any bears Monty *wasn't* related too?

At last, the ambulance stopped and the engine cut off. After a moment, the back doors opened and Mr Crankly appeared again. He'd parked by the steps that led down to the canal.

Monty and Patrick climbed out. Monty lumbered straight down the steps to the water, which was good as the canal path couldn't be seen from the road.

Mr Crankly and Patrick made their way down the steps.

Monty stood on the canal path. He sniffed the air, his white fur glinting in the moonlight.

Patrick couldn't believe they'd made it.

'Well, I guess you'd best get going,' Mr Crankly said to Monty.

'Indeed I must,' Monty said, looking along the canal.

'I checked the Port of London Authority website. There's a boat departing at five, and another at seven if you miss that one. Just in case the river trout aren't aware.'

Monty nodded at Mr Crankly. 'Thank you for the information, old chap. Most useful. Although I do find the trout to be rather reliable.'

Mr Crankly stepped forward. 'Cheerio,' he said, holding out his hand to Monty.

Monty clasped Mr Crankly's hand between his paws. 'Yes, cheerio, Clifford, old sport. Do come and visit. The Arctic is

352

splendid at any time of year, and I'm always up for a game of chess.'

Mr Crankly smiled.

Patrick felt a lump forming in his throat. He was finding it difficult to look at Monty. He didn't want him to go. Buying enough tinned sardines for Monty, keeping him in the garage, and worrying about how he was going to get him home, had been hard. Despite all this, he still wondered if there was a way for Monty to stay.

He knew there wasn't.

Patrick felt his eyes growing wet. He sniffed and wiped them with the sleeve of his coat. Monty had been his friend, a funny sort of friend, but a friend nonetheless. He was going to miss him.

Monty smiled kindly and held out his paw. 'I'll be seeing you, old bean. Don't forget me.'

Patrick rushed forward and threw his arms around Monty. His fur was soft and warm

353

and smelled of bear, of *Monty*. He let out a loud sob.

Monty patted Patrick's back whilst holding him close in a hug. 'Now, now. No need to be upset, old chum. I'm just an ordinary bear.' Monty released Patrick. 'You know where I live, don't you?'

Patrick nodded through his tears. 'Greenland.'

'Not quite.' Monty placed a paw on Patrick's heart. 'Here, old sport. I live here.'

Patrick tried to smile even though his eyes were full of tears.

Monty then placed his paw over his own heart. 'And you live right here, my dearest chum. You always will.'

Patrick felt overwhelmed with love for that funny old bear. He was going to miss Monty so much. He had always known what to say. A single tear slid down Patrick's nose.

Mr Crankly handed Patrick a clean

handkerchief which Patrick used to wipe his eyes with.

Monty stood at the edge of the canal. 'Take good care, chaps. Remember, freedom, books, flowers and the moon.'

'And a tin of condensed milk,' Patrick managed to say.

'That's the spirit,' Monty said, giving them both a big wave. 'We don't need much to be happy.'

'Aye,' said Mr Crankly who seemed to be struggling to get his own words out.

With that Monty dropped into the canal making

a splash. His head appeared above the water. 'Farewell, dear friends.'

'Cheerio,' Mr Crankly said, sniffing a little.

'Goodbye,' Patrick whispered.

Mr Crankly took another handkerchief from his dressing gown pocket and dabbed at his own eyes. He put his hand on Patrick's shoulder and they watched as Monty disappeared under the water. There were a few ripples and then nothing. The night was still and cold, the water dark and empty.

Another tear slide down Patrick's nose and onto the path.

They stood for a minute or two, neither of them wanting to leave.

'Look there, Private Jolly.' Mr Crankly was pointing.

They looked along the canal. Monty's head was rising slowly out of the water, a small white dot against the black night. He

356

smiled, lifted a paw and waved. Patrick and Mr Crankly waved back.

Monty turned, and then he was gone, his head disappearing under the water for the last time.

Patrick brushed away his tears.

'He certainly wasn't an ordinary bear,' Mr Crankly said.

'He was one of a kind,' Patrick agreed.

They walked up the steps to the ambulance. There no longer seemed any urgency. Everything felt different without Monty.

This time Patrick climbed into the cab next to Mr Crankly.

'Time to get you home,' Mr Crankly said, starting the engine. 'Let's hope no one's missed you, eh?'

'I hope not,' Patrick said. 'I'll be grounded until I'm forty if they've noticed I'm missing.' He was trying to be cheerful but it was hard. He still had that lump in his throat.

Mr Crankly chuckled. 'Quite right. Although it isn't every day you complete an operation like this, sending a polar bear home to Greenland. This is what you would call *extraordinary circumstances*.'

Patrick had to agree. Nothing had been ordinary since Monty had arrived.

As they drove, he thought about the journey Monty had to make and how exciting it would be. Perhaps a little scary at times. Patrick was sure Monty would be okay because Monty was that sort of bear.

Patrick was glad he was going home now too, to his house, his bedroom and Mr Nutkins, to everything he knew and loved, and to his parents who loved him *and* each other.

He knew how lucky he was.

Outside, it began to snow. Large, fat flakes fell from the sky, landing on the road ahead and the windscreen.

'Snow,' Patrick said. 'Mr Carson was right. Maybe we'll get a snow day.'

Mr Crankly put the wipers on and turned the heater up.

'I almost forgot, Private Jolly, I owe you a football.'

'What?'

'You kicked a ball into my garden once and when I tried to kick it back over to you, it landed on my railing.' Mr Crankly grinned. 'I was never much good at football.'

'Thanks,' Patrick said. 'It's really no big deal – about the ball. It was an old one.'

'All the same, you'll be getting a new one. It's on my to-do list, along with filling in the pond. I was never fond of those fish. Susan wanted them. I'm so pleased the heron got them.'

Patrick smiled.

At last, they pulled into Cherry Tree Close. Mr Crankly turned the ambulance lights off and parked quietly over the road from Patrick's house.

'Good work tonight, Private Jolly. See you soon, I hope.'

'Are you really going now?' Patrick asked.

'I'm afraid so. Got to get this back before she's missed or needed. Got to get myself back too – before they realise my bed's empty.' Mr Crankly chuckled to himself. 'Feel free to pop over for a lemonade and a ginger biscuit when I'm home.'

'I will.' And he meant it. Maybe he'd even try and learn to play chess.

He opened the door and jumped out of the ambulance. Cherry Tree Close was dark and quiet but also familiar and comforting. 'Mission accomplished,' Patrick whispered, before shutting the ambulance door.

Mr Crankly saluted him, then started the engine. He set off, driving slowly along the road.

Patrick stood waving, the snowflakes melting on the pavement and on his coat sleeves. The half moon shone down on Cherry Tree Close. The falling snow was illuminated under the light of the lamppost.

He crossed the road and stepped onto his drive, digging his key out of his coat pocket.

Monty had been nothing but trouble. Still, he knew he was really going to miss that bear.

Emily Critchley

Emily grew up in Essex. She has lived in Brighton, London, and now lives in Hertfordshire. She has a BA in Creative Writing from London Metropolitan University and an MA in Creative Writing from Birkbeck, University of London. Her YA debut *Notes on my Family* was nominated for the Carnegie, book of the week in *The Sunday Times* and long listed for the Branford Boase.

Praise for *Notes on my Family*
Emily's debut for YA

'This exceptional young adult/crossover debut is the compelling, sharply observed story of a family in crisis told, in an understated narrative voice reminiscent of Mark Haddon or Harper Lee, by 13-year-old Lou, who is on the autism spectrum.'

The Sunday Times, Book of the Week

'A warm, witty and moving look at one complicated family and the girl at the heart of it. Full of sincerity, intelligence and hope.'

Anna James, *A Case for Books*

'A compelling story with nuanced characters who leap off the page. Brilliantly observed.'

Julia Bell, author of *The Dark Light*